PRIDE AND PREJUDICE AND MISTLETOE

ALSO BY MELISSA DE LA CRUZ

ST. MARTIN'S GRIFFIN
NEW YORK

PRIDE
AND
PREJUDICE
AND
MISTLETOE

MELISSA
DE LA CRUZ

PRIDE AND PREJUDICE AND MISTLETOE. Copyright © 2017 by Melissa de la Cruz. All rights reserved. Printed in the United States of America. For information, address St. Martin's Press, 175 Fifth Avenue, New York, N.Y. 10010.

www.stmartins.com

Designed by Anna Gorovoy

The Library of Congress has cataloged the hardcover edition as follows:

Names: De la Cruz, Melissa, 1971– author.
Title: Pride and prejudice and mistletoe / Melissa de la Cruz.
Description: First U.S. edition. | New York : St. Martin's Press, 2017.
Identifiers: LCCN 2017023633 | ISBN 9781250141392 (hardcover) |
    ISBN 9781250164827 (international, sold outside the U.S., subject to
    rights availability) | ISBN 9781250141408 (ebook)
Subjects: LCSH: Christmas stories. | GSAFD: Love stories.
Classification: LCC PS3604.E128 P75 2017 | DDC 813/.6—dc23
LC record available at https://lccn.loc.gov/2017023633

ISBN 978-1-250-18946-2 (trade paperback)

Our books may be purchased in bulk for promotional, educational, or business use. Please contact your local bookseller or the Macmillan Corporate and Premium Sales Department at 1-800-221-7945, extension 5442, or by email at MacmillanSpecialMarkets@macmillan.com.

First St. Martin's Griffin Edition: October 2018

10 9 8 7 6 5 4 3 2 1

For Mike and Mattie, always

ACKNOWLEDGMENTS

I am so grateful to the following people for making this book a reality: my editors, Brenda Copeland and Sara Goodman at St. Martin's; my agents, Richard Abate and Rachel Kim at 3Arts; and especially Brad Krevoy and Amanda Phillips at Brad Krevoy Television. Thank you to all my friends and family.

1

A Taylor Swift cover of "Last Christmas," originally recorded by Wham! in 1986, strummed from the stereo of the sleek, black town car, where Darcy was sitting in the backseat. Over the driver's seat she could see Edward's head bobbing up and down as they drove over the bumpy terrain, and it was somewhat of a comfort. Edward had worked for the Fitzwilliam family since Darcy was a small girl, and though she told herself over and over that she hadn't missed anything about her hometown in the eight years since she'd fled, the truth was she *had* missed Edward. Despite being only fifteen years older than she was, he had a grandfatherly twinkle in his blue eyes and an impressively sharp memory that she had always admired. He always remembered everything she told him. And she told him plenty, as he was the only person in her family she felt she could trust.

"She's going to be okay," Edward said from the front seat. "So you can wipe that worried look off your face, my dear."

"Oh, I hope you're right," she said, chewing her bottom lip anxiously. "But you know how my mom is. She'll never let people know if she's suffering."

"That's true." She watched his head bob up and down. "You know, you haven't aged one bit," he said, looking at her reflection in the rearview mirror.

"I know." She tried to smile through her nerves. "You always told me if I kept scowling I'd have forehead wrinkles by twenty-five."

"Now you're twenty-nine and wrinkle free!" He chuckled. "What's your secret, *Miss Fitzwilliam*?"

He never called her that. Darcy, Darce, the Darcinator, sometimes Darce-Tastic, but never Miss Fitzwilliam—that was her mother's name. Doing so now was a playful acknowledgment of the way she'd skyrocketed to a position of unfathomable power and status, in the time since he'd last seen her, that even her own blue-blooded family had never quite held. He was proud of her, she could tell, and she appreciated it. At least *somebody* from her old life was.

She swallowed hard, so unsure of how she'd be received in her family home. How should she act when she saw them all again? How did she *used to* act around them? Suddenly she couldn't remember; suddenly she felt seized by anxiety, like this one interaction with her parents and brothers after eight years would make or break their relationship for the entire future.

From the outside, anyone would think that Darcy Fitzwilliam was doing unusually well on her own in New York City, and in many ways she was. But in her gut she knew something was horribly off, and when she'd got that middle-of-the-night phone call, she finally knew what was missing. Her glamorous Manhattan life was missing family, people to love and to be loved by. She'd hopped on the first flight home. Now, for the sake of at least making a good impression on Edward, she used all her energy to shake off the nervousness and said, "My secret? A lady never reveals her secrets, *Mister Peterson*."

She turned then to face her reflection. It was true: at twenty-nine and as partner at the second most successful hedge fund in NYC, she didn't look a day over twenty-four. She was confident in her good looks and considered herself to be just as gorgeous as everybody told her she was. Her slender, heart-shaped face boasted elegantly chiseled cheekbones; a lightly freckled, ski-slope nose; big, stormy gray eyes shuttered by naturally long lashes; and a perfectly pouty set of pale pink lips. Now and then she started to think they were losing their youthful luster, and in those moments she'd briefly toy with the idea of getting them plumped. But the thought was always fleeting, as she had far more important things on her mind. The real question for Darcy was not to plump or not to plump. No, it was something far less simple and far more troubling.

See, it is a truth universally acknowledged that any beautiful, brilliant, single woman who is rich as hell will be in want of a husband. She'd heard it time and time again.

"But Darcy, you could have any man in Manhattan!" her closest friend, Kate Myles, would despair from time to time. "Just pick the sexiest one and marry him."

"*Marry* him?" Audrey Rooney, their third musketeer, would balk. "How about she starts by going on a *date* with him? The girl probably hasn't seen a naked man in a decade. She could use a little fun."

Darcy would just sit back and watch her friends assess her love life back and forth like a tennis match. That was back when she had time for friends.

And she'd get it from strangers, too. Cocktail party attendees and cabdrivers and doctors and reporters and TV repairmen and waiters and salespeople all wanted to know the answer to one question: *Why are you—how are you—still single?* And the question on Darcy's mind: *Why don't I care?*

When, from time to time, she had a few spare hours to analyze and assess her life, she would realize that it wasn't that she didn't ever care to settle down and get married; it was that she had less than zero interest in doing these things with anyone who didn't make her heart absolutely melt. The way Darcy saw it, she'd have real passionate love or she would have none at all. Of course she preferred the thought of the former, but without it, she was prepared to settle on the latter. Anybody who perceived Darcy as coldhearted and callous had misunderstood her. The truth was that beneath her cool exterior was a very warm, very willing heart, waiting patiently to give itself to the right person. She just hadn't found him yet.

The car wound through the dense woods of Pemberley, Ohio, light filtering through the skinny, shivering tree branches onto the gravelly road beneath them. They exited the woods and turned onto a quaint though elegant street lined with quintessentially Midwestern homes, followed by a quintessentially Midwestern church placed at the end of the street like a period at the end of a sentence. From there they turned onto a new street, a broader one, with homes that became increasingly grand in size and stature, and increasingly farther and farther apart. And at the very end of that road, where the street ended in the most expansive cul-de-sac you could imagine, was the Fitzwilliam mansion, looming not unlike a luxury ocean liner. The Fitzwilliam home was rusty brick red with one massive, round, white portico and two rows of twelve dormer windows. Elaborately conical topiary lined the cobblestone path leading up to the tall, black lacquered door. Darcy held her breath as they approached, trying not to think of the last time she'd walked out of that same door. Had it been a mistake? One she wouldn't ever be able to take back?

Edward parked the car and walked around to the back to open Darcy's door for her.

"You can relax, Darce," he said. "They'll all be happy to see you."

Darcy nodded and walked up the cobblestone steps. She held her finger a half inch away from the pearlescent doorbell for several seconds, then pressed it quickly, before she had any more time to think.

The door swung open almost immediately and there stood Lorna Sheppard, the elderly housekeeper. She nodded her graying head formally at Darcy, welcoming her in.

"So good to see you, Miss Fitzwilliam," she said kindly. "It's been too long."

"How is she?" Darcy blurted. She wanted to throw her arms around Lorna, who had practically raised her, but she worried that if she did so she might break down and cry on the spot, right then and there in the resplendent foyer, and that would just be unproductive.

"Stable, dear," Lorna replied. "It will make her feel quite a deal better, knowing you'll be home for Christmas for once."

Darcy looked up and saw the gigantic wreath hanging above the symmetrically curved, double staircases. Christmas. For the past eight years she had lived in New York, all Christmas had meant was dry martinis and lavish office parties where she'd spend an hour or two swatting away the advances of much older men and trying not to look as bitter and grim as she felt. It meant nightly window-shopping extravaganzas on Fifth Avenue, which turned into actual shopping extravaganzas, during which she'd drop thousands on designer bags and shoes and glasses and gloves and jewelry, then take it all home and try it all on and fall asleep, alone, in front of *Shark Tank* reruns. She couldn't remember the last time she'd spent Christmas Day with someone.

Actually, she didn't have a great memory of any of the past eight Christmases at all. As far as she had been concerned, Christmas alone as the third-wealthiest woman under twenty-nine in New York was a freebie day, a twenty-four-hour period in which she could do as she pleased, and so she started with the martinis sometime around ten in the morning and kept them coming until the next day, when it was time to sober up for work.

And now here she was, dragged back home for the holidays, just like she never wanted to be. Wanting to be near family and actually being near family were two completely different things. But standing here now, she found herself wondering what she'd been so afraid of.

"Is she upstairs?" Darcy asked.

"Yes, in the master bedroom."

"And my dad?"

"He's with her. Hasn't left her side."

"Of course not." Darcy forced a smile and slipped awkwardly past Lorna.

She made her way up the stairs. The banisters were looped with festive gold ribbon and shimmery lametta; real poinsettia berries and fresh mistletoe were hanging from the chandeliers and door frames. Her life in New York was filled with plenty of luxuries and frills, but nothing like this. In New York there wasn't enough room for such extravagant displays of wealth, and so the displays were restricted to a smaller space. As she strolled down the hallway to her parents' bedroom, she took it all in—the baroque sconces and framed portraits of generations of Fitzwilliams, the ice-blue damask wallpaper and ceilings so high they looked like one big, never-ending, open white void—as if seeing it for the first time.

When she came to the end of the hallway, she knocked lightly on the door, the same door she used to knock on in the middle of the night if woken by a nightmare or an unusual noise.

"Who's there?" came her father's voice from the other side.

"It's Darcy."

Silence. Murmuring. Footsteps. Finally, the door opened, and she found herself face-to-face with her dad, John B. Fitzwilliam, looking just as stern and somber as ever, only now with what seemed to Darcy a look of disappointment and resentment layered on top. She gulped. Not much frightened Darcy Fitzwilliam, but her father definitely did.

"Well, well," he said. "Look who it is."

"Johnny, be nice to her." This voice came from Darcy's mother, who lay in a canopy bed, white as paper. A young nurse, maybe in her early twenties, stood by her side, and looked up to smile at Darcy.

Darcy awkwardly circled around her dad and power walked clumsily to the bed. She took her mom's hand in her own.

"Mom!" she laugh-cried. "A heart attack? At sixty-five? You had me worried sick."

"I tell her to fix up her diet," Mr. Fitzwilliam mumbled. "She won't give up those beignets."

"I'm fine. I'm fine." Mrs. Fitzwilliam smiled. "It's all just a ploy to get my baby girl home for the holidays."

"Very funny, Mom." Darcy patted Mrs. Fitzwilliam's hand and sat down by her side. "You know I've just been so . . . busy. I'm—"

"Yes, we know," Mr. Fitzwilliam interrupted, then stared past her silently. She could imagine what he was thinking: *You're partner at the second-largest hedge fund in New York City, you're practically a princess, you don't have one single weekend or holiday to spare for your family.*

"John," Mrs. Fitzwilliam scolded, "I told you to be nice. You'll give me another heart attack!"

"Well I'm sorry, dear, but it's hard to be nice at a time like this." He held his head high, unwilling to look Darcy in the eye. Darcy thought this quite childish but kept the opinion to herself.

"Darcy." Mrs. Fitzwilliam looked up at her daughter. "I am so relieved to have you here, and I know how busy you've been."

Darcy hadn't been home in eight years, but that hadn't been the last time she'd seen her mom. Mrs. Fitzwilliam didn't hold the same grudge against her daughter as Mr. Fitzwilliam did, and so she had flown to New York City on three different occasions. The first time: when Darcy broke up with her college boyfriend, Carl. The second time: when Darcy was hospitalized due to stress and lack of sleep. The third time: when Darcy was made partner of Montrose and Montrose, thus making it Montrose Montrose and Fitzwilliam. It had been a full year, and she realized, as she sat down at her mother's side, just how much she had missed her. She had nothing to do with Darcy's estrangement, after all. As far as Darcy was concerned, she was one of the good guys.

"You're here just in time for the party." Mrs. Fitzwilliam spoke softly, as if trying to save her voice.

"What party?" Darcy asked.

"We'll see if you're even well enough to throw a party," Mr. Fitzwilliam cautioned.

"I told you, I'm fine. Even Dr. Law says I'm fine," Mrs. Fitzwilliam insisted. "And it's not like we can cancel on two hundred people, can we?"

"We can do whatever we want when it comes to preserving your health," he replied.

"What party?" Darcy asked again.

"The annual Christmas party!" Just saying these words seemed to bring a delighted rosy color to her mom's cheeks. "You didn't think we had all these decorations strung up just for ourselves, did you?"

"No, I guess not," Darcy said, feeling her hands grow sweaty.

"What's wrong?" Mrs. Fitzwilliam asked. "You used to love our Christmas parties."

"Yeah, when I was a kid." Darcy's fight-or-flight response was starting to kick in. "But I'm just . . . I'm not prepared for a party. I don't have anything to wear."

"You don't have anything to wear?" Mr. Fitzwilliam laughed sourly. "You're Darcy Fitzwilliam. Go to Bloomingdale's; it's less than a mile away."

Darcy stuttered, "Oh, okay, but the thing is . . ." No matter how hard she tried, she couldn't think of a good excuse for not being able to make it to the party. She had flown all the way out to the middle of nowhere (or so it seemed, compared to New York), and everyone knew she didn't have any other plans.

"Yes?" Mr. Fitzwilliam raised his eyebrows at her.

"Okay, yeah," she gave in. "Of course. I'll get a dress."

Mrs. Fitzwilliam clapped her hands together. "I'm so happy, it's almost like I didn't have a heart attack!"

"But you did," Mr. Fitzwilliam reminded her. "So let's try not to get too excited just yet."

"All right, all right." Mrs. Fitzwilliam took a deep, calming breath. "Darcy, sweetheart, I know you've just traveled a long way. Maybe you'd like to take a bit to get settled? Maybe an afternoon nap would be nice."

"I can have Lorna show you to your room," Mr. Fitzwilliam added.

"Um." Darcy was confused for a moment. "Why would I need her to show me where my room is?"

"Well, it *has* been quite a long time."

"I see." Darcy quietly took in the jab. "I think I'll be just fine. But thanks for your concern, Dad."

He gestured to the door as if to say *Then go*. There had been a part of her that thought maybe, after all these years, there was no way he could still be so mad, or so hurt, whichever it was. She closed the door behind her thinking, *I guess I was wrong.* Time, so far, hadn't healed this wound.

2

Darcy's childhood bedroom was half a floor beneath her parents' and on the end of a marble landing. It overlooked an Olympic-size swimming pool surrounded by checkerboard tile and white lounge chairs, with an infinity waterfall segueing into a clear blue hot tub. The room hadn't changed one bit since she had last seen it eight years ago. The navy sateen of her canopy bed, the wall of plaques and trophies from high school debates and academic honors and horseback riding competitions. It was all still there. She locked the door behind her and went to her bookshelf, which still held all her old favorite books: *The Great Gatsby, Atlas Shrugged, Sense and Sensibility, War and Peace,* and so many more. These had been the books to get her through the loneliness of high school. She ran her finger along their spines.

"Oh my God." She laughed, her eyes falling on the stuffed animal perched at the end of the shelf. "Little Lion!" Little Lion had been a present from her father when she was nine years old and had to have her appendix removed. She could still remember waking up from surgery to find her father at the side of the bed, holding the stuffed animal with a red bow around its neck, made extra bright and shimmery by the painkillers. She had named him Little Lion because, even then, she didn't like the idea of making things up. She liked cold, hard facts that couldn't be argued with, and so she gave him a name that would most accurately represent who he was.

Now she took him in her arms and laid down on the cool cotton sheets of her childhood bed. As she lay there, the sun began to set outside the wide window, where freshly cut flowers sat in Le Creuset vases. And as the sun set, her thoughts spun. It had been a whirlwind twelve hours since she received the phone call with news of her mother's heart attack and she hopped on the first morning flight to Ohio. The transition from her new life suddenly into her old life felt surreal and jarring. She couldn't reconcile the person she was now with the person she used to be, and she couldn't get the image of her father's disappointed, resentful face out of her head.

At the same time that her old life felt light-years away, it was also hard to believe that it had been eight whole years since things had gone sour between her and her father. In some ways, it felt like just yesterday that she had "let her whole family and community down" by not agreeing to follow her father's plan for her. What he wanted was for her to marry her high school (and on-and-off-again college) boyfriend, Carl, who came from a respectable family of lawyers, doctors, and war heroes who had been the pride and joy of Pemberley, Ohio, for generations. Darcy had tried hard to feel passionate about Carl, tried to convince herself that he was the one, but at the end of the day their days together felt dry and their nights left much to be desired. Mr. Fitzwilliam's wishes for his daughter were twofold, and the second fold involved her doing what a truly good and honorable woman would do: give birth to children and dedicate her life to raising them. Like the first fold of his plan, this didn't work for her either.

"I don't *have* to marry him, Dad," she had said, sitting across from him at the long, stretching dining room table.

"No, you don't," he had replied triumphantly, as if the card he held would surely win this game. "Not if you don't mind living on your own money."

"You mean—"

"That's right. I'll restrict you from access to your inheritance, and I certainly won't finance your life while you gallivant around New York City doing Lord knows what."

Darcy had considered this momentarily, but ultimately knew what she had to do. Her happiness was in jeopardy, after all. She rejected her family money, broke up with Carl for the dozenth time, and moved to New York in search of what it meant to be independent.

"We made the right decision, didn't we, Little Lion?" Sometimes she wasn't so sure. After all, this was her first Christmas with people other than herself, and here she was talking to a stuffed lion, the only thing she had ever truly been able to confide in. It wasn't that she didn't have any friends; it was just that nobody could understand her the way an inanimate, nonresponsive object could.

"You're pathetic," she said to herself, then apologized for the insult. Her therapist, Dr. Springs, liked to talk to her about self-love and going easy on oneself, something Darcy knew almost nothing about. In the way of self-care, all Darcy really knew was setting goals and working toward them, then rewarding or punishing herself depending on the outcome.

"Don't beat yourself up," Dr. Springs liked to say. "You can't pour from an empty cup. Take care of yourself first, otherwise you'll have nothing to work with."

She repeated these messages in her head, telling herself that she'd have to relax and put her life back in New York aside if she wanted to be of any real help to her mom at all. Her mom would be okay, wouldn't she? If Mrs. Fitzwilliam was telling the truth, then she was on the mend and would be good as new by Christmas. This would be a onetime thing and life would go on as usual. But Darcy knew all about her mom's bad habits and faltering health. She'd been a lifelong smoker, had a sweet tooth the size of Mount Everest, and was one of those women who made it look glamorous to start drinking Belvedere at ten in the morning. When Darcy had held her hand upstairs, it had felt cold and frail. A small wave of fear rolled through the pit of Darcy's stomach.

She unzipped her Louis Vuitton suitcase and took out her favorite Kate Spade deco dot pajamas. She took out her toothbrush and the lavender-scented, self-cooling eye mask that she never slept without. As she carried these items to bed, she felt exhaustion rise up as if from nowhere to claim her. It closed in around her foggy head, causing her eyelids to droop suddenly. *I'll just sit down for one minute*, she thought, letting the weight of her body plop down onto the bedding. She let her eyes close, and before she had time to protest, she fell asleep, clutching her belongings to her chest.

The next morning, Darcy woke, startled and disoriented, at the first sign of sunlight. *Where am I?* she wondered for a brief moment, before the reality of waking life came flooding back. There was a knock at her door.

"Who is it?" she called out.

"Lorna, dear."

"Just a second!" Darcy looked down at her fully clothed self. She tore off her clothes and slipped into the Kate Spade pajamas, not wanting word to get around that she had fallen asleep in her clothes. "Okay, you can come in," she said, once she felt presentable, more like a civilized human being and less like the sleep-deprived workaholic she was.

The door opened and there stood Lorna with a silver breakfast tray, supplied with a pot of steaming-hot coffee and a sprig of honeysuckle.

"You didn't have to do that!" Darcy insisted, standing up to meet Lorna halfway.

"Your mother insisted," Lorna said, brushing off Darcy's attempt to help her and setting the silver tray down on Darcy's nightstand.

"How is she doing?" Darcy sat cross-legged on the bed and picked up an orange from the tray.

"Honestly, dear, she's not doing very well. Nothing to worry about, really, but Dr. Law doesn't want her going to the party tonight. He thinks it's better she rest. Gather her strength."

"Lucky," Darcy said, before she could stop herself.

"Sorry, dear?" Lorna looked alarmed.

"Oh, ha," Darcy scrambled to explain, "of course I didn't mean she's lucky to be ill. I just meant that I myself am sort of . . . uncomfortable about going to the party, so I meant my mom is lucky that she has a good excuse not to go. I didn't mean for it to be insensitive. I'm worried about her, of course, I hate to think—"

"Darcy." Lorna's tone was gentle, warm, and forgiving. "I've known you long enough to know that you're anything but insensitive."

"Really? Most people think I'm a coldhearted bitch. Excuse my language."

"Well, those people don't know the real you. They only know your tough exterior you've developed from years of having to fend for yourself. But I've known you since you were a baby, don't forget. You can't fool me."

"Well, thank you, Lorna," Darcy said earnestly. "That means a lot to me."

"You're very welcome. Now, why don't you want to go to this party?"

"The same reason I never come home!" Darcy explained, throwing her hands up. "Because half the people in this town take it as a personal offense that I left! And they're all going to be at the party. Not to mention my own dad, who uses every opportunity he possibly can to try to make me feel bad for leaving. And if my mom's not well enough to go to the party, why should I? She's the whole reason I'm here, isn't she? I should stay upstairs with her and keep her company."

"First of all, your mother knew you would say that, and she wants me to tell you that she insists you attend the party. She's been wanting you at an annual Christmas party for eight years, and now that you're here, she won't take no for an answer."

"What? Why?"

"*Because*," Lorna explained, "she wants you to reconnect with the people who love you, the place where you came from."

"Oh boy." Darcy rolled her eyes, but she had a gnawing feeling that her mother was right, that maybe she actually could benefit from reconnecting to her roots. Pemberley wasn't perfect, and she'd had her reasons to flee, but living here she'd never been half as lonely as she was in New York. Her life back in Pemberley had been slower, sure, but it had feeling, it had substance. It had late-night conversations at the Tavern and all-day picnics in the fall. And, lastly, her life in Pemberley had familiar faces with good intentions, people who knew her and always wanted what was best for her, even though they never understood her, not really.

"Now, second of all, I hope you don't take this the wrong way, but besides your father, nobody cares that you left. They're all over it. They have their own lives to worry about. And nobody thinks you're a freak; they're all too busy thinking about themselves to think of you at all."

"Lorna!" Darcy laughed.

"It's true, dear. Nobody blames you for leaving home and following your dreams. If anything, you're probably respected for it by now."

"I hope you're right, Lorna." Darcy smiled.

3

Darcy descended the spiral staircase at five thirty in the afternoon, not a second earlier than she had to. She had reluctantly taken her dad's advice to go shopping at Bloomingdale's and was now wearing an Herve Leger cocktail dress with an open back and a tight fit. Perfectly hugging and outlining her slender curves, it was just the right amount of provocative. Trying to make the sale, the shopgirl had emphasized the words "deep-sea blue" and "flirty cutout," but Darcy hadn't needed any convincing. She had swiped her Amex without trying on the dress.

The entertainment hall was decked floor to ceiling in silver and gold, and the waitstaff bustled around in black and white. The guests, who grew in number by the minute, held champagne flutes and china teacups filled to the brim with eggnog, greeting one another with practiced delight and forced excitement that echoed throughout the great room. Darcy zigzagged through the crowd, nodding at vaguely familiar faces she hadn't seen in a decade and dodging those that were more familiar, who she was more comfortable avoiding. If she were to spend a whole night talking to people she didn't want to talk to, and do so without dwelling on the fact that her mom was weak and recovering from a heart attack that very well could have killed her, she would need to start on the eggnog ASAP. It was nice to revisit home and to be with her mother, who she adored, but every hour away from work was an anxious one for Darcy, and there was nothing she hated more than being stuck around people she knew probably gossiped about her behind her back. *It's December nineteenth*, she said to herself. *You'll be out of here by Christmas. You can do this.*

She found the bar and ordered her first drink of the night. The milky bourbon warmed her throat and spread through her body in comforting, tingly waves. Just as she took that first gulp, she looked up and saw Chris Mayfair—who had been her first kiss, among other firsts, in the ninth grade—striding toward her with a big grin on his face.

Darcy had been single for almost six years by this point, but that didn't mean she hadn't had her fair share of boyfriends, not to mention a fair share of broken hearts she'd left behind. Chris had always been handsome, but now, as he approached her, he looked more picture perfect than ever before, a tan, toned, chiseled specimen of a man who looked like he had walked straight out of a Ralph Lauren catalog and into the Fitzwilliam Christmas party.

"Look who it is!" He pulled Darcy in for a hug as if they'd stayed close throughout all these years.

"Chris! Hi!" She put on her best smile, even as she recoiled from his embrace. It wasn't that she didn't like Chris; it was just that she was cagey around anyone who was so quintessentially Pemberley. The crew cut, the cardigan, the Colgate-white teeth. She had called things off with him at the end of ninth grade because of his unappealing passion for baseball and the fact that he was, when all was said and done, a dull conversationalist.

"I can't believe how long it's been. How's New York treating you?"

"It's, uh . . . it's pretty great, actually. I'm—"

"You know, I've always wanted to go to the Big Apple. See a show on Broadway. I heard they have an ice cream parlor where you can get bowls of ice cream as big as your head. Is that true?"

"It's true." She nodded, trying not to grimace. "Serendipity."

"It is like serendipity, bumping into you after all this time."

"No, I meant . . . that's the name of the ice cream parlor."

"Annie! Over here!" He wasn't listening to her anymore, but instead was waving over a pretty blond woman with an elegant giraffe neck, who looked lost in the crowd, helpless as a deer in the headlights. She saw Chris and slipped through the growing crowd toward him. Once she was standing there, Darcy could see the blinding diamond on her finger and the pregnant curve of her stomach.

"Darcy, this is my wife, Annie." He beamed, putting his arm around her. "Annie, this is Darcy."

"*The* Darcy?" she asked, extending her hand for Darcy to shake. "I've heard so much about you."

"You have?"

"But of course she has," said Chris. "You're Darcy Fitz-william! Not only the only Pemberley High graduate to leave home, but the only one to make it big all on her own. You're the only one of us not living off Daddy's dime, as far as I know. Not to mention you're the only one of us who, you know, hasn't settled down."

"*Very* admirable." Annie nodded, though the tone in her voice suggested she didn't find it admirable as much as pitiful.

"Ah." Darcy smiled graciously, then tried to change the subject. "So, you're having a baby! Congratulations!" She took a sip of her eggnog.

"It's our fourth, actually," Chris informed her proudly.

"And our first girl!" Annie added.

"Fourth?" Darcy balked, almost spitting out her drink.

"Yes!" the couple cheered in unison.

"You've been raising three boys? I can't imagine how you have time for—"

"Oh, well, we have *help*," Annie interjected. "It's not so hard when you have help."

"Of course." Darcy finished off her eggnog.

"And Annie stays home with them," Chris chimed in. "It's not like she has to work."

"Of course." Darcy nodded along, trying not to look like she wanted nothing more than to disappear into thin air.

"When do you think you'll start a family?" Annie asked earnestly. "It truly is the most rewarding experience. And I know a lot of people say that, and you're like 'Well, that can't be true,' but it is; it really is. I wouldn't trade it for the world."

"Well, isn't that lovely?" Darcy gave her a thin smile. "I'm just not quite there yet. Things are really busy at work, and I don't exactly have a man lined up."

"Oh." Annie looked concerned. "But you've started thinking

about it, haven't you? We women don't have all the time in the world, unfortunately."

"Why *are* you still single?" Chris asked. "You were always so popular with the boys." Darcy wasn't sure if she could detect a hint of gloating in his voice or if it was only in her imagination.

"Maybe I've lost my charm!" She laughed awkwardly. Annie and Chris just blinked. "Excuse me," she said. "I think it's time for a second drink."

4

The eggnog was strong enough to get her through an average Christmas party, but the night was young and this party was already shaping up to be anything but average. So she ordered bourbon on the rocks and did her best to stay invisible. She saw her twenty-one-year-old brother, James, arrive with his fiancée, Michelle, then saw her seventeen-year-old brother, William, arrive with what must have been his girlfriend du jour, and made a quick break for the stairs, deciding she'd hide out with her mom for the rest of the evening, whether she was welcome there or not.

"Darcy!" It wasn't her brother's voice. In fact, it was the only voice she wanted to hear. She turned around to see Bingley Charles, her very best friend from high school and college.

"Oh my God, Bingley!" She jumped off the stairs and tackled

him with a tipsy hug. He hugged her back, and they stood there embracing for several seconds.

"I can't believe you're here!" He shoved her playfully.

"Me? I can't believe *you're* here!"

"Well, I'm here every year. Haven't missed a single Fitzwilliam Christmas party."

"Really?" She was shocked. "*Why?*"

"Unlike you, I come home for the holidays. Your mom has always sent me an invitation, so I make an appearance."

After college, Bingley had moved to Los Angeles to pursue a career in acting, and she hadn't seen him since.

"I had no idea." She stared, wondering how she could have become *that* disconnected from her best friend.

"How would you? You're too busy being one of the most powerful women in New York City!" He grinned warmly. "You know, when most people call their friends that, they don't mean it literally."

"Oh stop." She tried to downplay her status, to not attract too much attention. "I'm not that powerful."

"That's not what *Forbes* magazine says," he reminded her. "They don't put just anyone on their covers, you know."

"You're too nice to me," she said. "You always have been."

"Well, you're one of the only people on this earth that I can stand, so most niceness goes to you by default."

They laughed, and Darcy squeezed his hand lovingly.

If Chris Mayfair was catalog model handsome, Bingley was movie star handsome. He had undeniably sculpted good looks, but unlike Chris, those looks came with character and personality, quirks and asymmetries that made his face just as lovable and unique as it was handsome.

"And . . ." Bingley surveyed the room with a grim glare. "From the looks of it, you're the only bearable human being at this party."

"Ditto."

"I guess we're stuck with each other for the night, then."

"I could think of much worse fates!" she said, sipping from her glass of bourbon and savoring the burn on her lips.

"Finish your drink so we can get eggnog," he advised. "Then we can sit back and judge everybody in the room like we did in college."

"Yes! Oh my God, remember the dance party at that eighties-themed bar? What was it called again?"

"Relax! With the exclamation point at the end and everything."

"That's right! An eighties-themed bar in Ohio. That was bleak."

"To say the least."

"And we were the only people who showed up in eighties clothes, and everyone was like . . . looking at us like we were freaks. And we were like 'Hel-lo-o, this is an *eighties-themed bar.*'" The bourbon was getting to her head, the buzz circulating like a loop of bees.

"So we bought water balloons and climbed up onto the roof of the building . . . Weird, I wonder how we got up there."

"And we threw them at anyone who wasn't wearing an eighties outfit!" Darcy laughed so hard at the memory that she snorted.

"Did you just snort, you animal?" Bingley teased her.

"Do you think it was mean of us to throw those balloons?" Darcy wondered out loud, still laughing, still trying to catch her breath.

"No! After they made fun of us for having some eighties spirit, we should have done a lot worse. Wish we had some water balloons right now, I can tell you that much," he joked.

"I can always count on you to clear my conscience," she said, downing the rest of her drink. "Now let's get some eggnog, babe."

They had only just ordered their eggnogs when Bingley tripped on a fallen Pottery Barn acorn.

"What the—" he exclaimed, as the liquid in his glass swished over the edge and sprayed onto the jacket sleeve of the man standing in front of them.

"Oops," Bingley said, and they giggled, too amused to be apologetic. But when the man turned around, Bingley fell silent and tried very hard to compose himself. This only made Darcy giggle harder.

"Jim!" Darcy laughed, realizing she knew this man. "I'm so sorry. Let's get you a new jacket. I'm sure there are plenty in the spare closet upstairs."

"Oh." The man named Jim looked down at his wet, milky sleeve and smiled. "Don't worry about it at all." He pulled a napkin off the nearest table and dabbed it on himself. "A little eggnog never hurt anyone. It's just so great to see you!" He went in for a hug from Darcy.

"It's been *way* too long," she said. "Jim, this is my friend Bingley Charles. Bingley, you remember our neighbor Jim Bennet, don't you?"

"I'm so sorry I got eggnog on you," Bingley said, blushing. "I tripped on that stupid acorn."

"Well then," Jim replied, looking Bingley straight in the eyes, "I don't blame you. I blame the acorn."

"Well, good luck getting it to apologize," Bingley said. "It's pretty stubborn, as far as acorns go."

Jim laughed, not breaking eye contact. Bingley smiled, pleased with himself. If Darcy knew Bingley at all, she knew he had a crush. Darcy would probably have had a crush on Jim, too, if she hadn't known that he was gay and would never go for a girl like Darcy anyway. Jim was grounded and centered; he valued service, education, and even a touch of spirituality. The last things he cared about were status, luxury, and vindication, the pillars on which Darcy thrived.

"Jim is a schoolteacher," Darcy said. "What grade do you teach, Jim, remind me?"

"Eighth grade."

"Wow, a teacher," said Bingley. "That's admirable work. Must be rewarding."

"It definitely *can* be. Eighth graders are tough, what with the hormones and discovery of marijuana and whatnot."

"I was a nightmare in eighth grade," Bingley admitted, summoning a look of mischief to his eyes, "for both those reasons."

Jim laughed again. *Wow*, thought Darcy, *Jim's into him, too.* Visions of matchmaking danced in her head.

"Will you excuse me?" She placed her hands on each of their shoulders. "I'm going to check on my mom, upstairs. Bingley, tell Jim about the screenplay you wanted to write. I'll be back in a flash."

She dipped away before either could protest. But when she turned back she saw that neither would have protested. In fact, neither seemed to notice that she had left.

Watching the two hit it off, instead of watching her step, and being more than slightly tipsy by this point, Darcy tripped and stumbled. She would have hit the floor, had she not been caught.

"Still klutzy as ever, I see," said the man who caught her. She looked up and, through the blur of alcohol, saw Luke Bennet. Luke was the older brother of Jim Bennet and had been Darcy's childhood archrival. Her cheeks burned when she realized it was his arms that were now cradling her close.

5

If Chris Mayfair was catalog handsome and Bingley was movie star handsome, then Luke was real-life-person handsome. He had dimples and dark brown eyes and his hair was never anything short of unruly. As a carpenter, he had strong arms that had always annoyed Darcy since they popped up in high school. They were what made him arrogant. He thought because he did work with his hands, which actually required real effort, that he was better than everyone else, and that was represented in his muscles. The problem was, she couldn't help but find them incredibly, incomparably sexy. The men she knew could play golf or win a debate or recite a limerick, but none could build, none could create, the way Luke could. And she *hated* that. She hated that he had this power over her. She swore she'd never let him know. He couldn't fully claim that power over her if he didn't know it existed.

"I am not a klutz," she protested, brushing herself off and taking a step back. "I'm just buzzed. As any sane person would be at a party like this." She was getting impatient with the night, the lengthening strand of awkward encounters.

"Hey, you don't have to tell me." He held up his mug of eggnog. "I'm on my fourth."

"Yes, but you've always been a lush." *Why am I being like this?* she scolded herself. *You're an adult. No need to push his buttons for absolutely no reason.* She couldn't explain it to herself or to anyone else, but something about him made her want to shake things up. Just him coming around had always made her feel as though she'd been startled awake out of a perfectly peaceful, oblivious sleep.

"Takes one to know one."

"Well then, I see you're just as *delightful* as ever," she said sarcastically. "Have a great night."

"Oh, come on, Darcy," he protested, "why do you have to take everything so seriously? I haven't seen you in, what, eight years? Let's catch up."

"Eight years, but not a minute too soon."

"Ouch. You're just mad because I caught you, literally, in a vulnerable moment."

"I'm not *vulnerable*." She stared in disbelief. How did such a holier-than-thou moron always know how to read her so well?

"No? You're home, where you hate to be, your mom is sick, and here you are at a party where everyone is happy with their lives, everyone is settled down. You stick out like a sore thumb."

"Oh, and I suppose you're so happy and settled?" Her heart

began to race. It was that surge of adrenaline she always imagined she'd feel when in love but so far had only ever felt during competition.

"Sure." He shrugged. "Can't complain."

"Hey, buddy," she laughed bitterly. "I'm not complaining either. I like my life exactly how it is. Not my problem that everyone wants me to settle down and start a family and blah blah blah. They're only jealous because I'm completely self-made, and a woman on top of that."

"They're *jealous*? Wow, I really know how to press your buttons, don't I?"

"You wish." She rolled her eyes, looking around for a way out of this fresh hell.

"I wish *what*, exactly?"

"That a nobody like you could affect somebody like me in any way whatsoever." She was drunk, she knew that now. She would never have said a thing like this sober. She might have thought it, but she wouldn't have *said* it. Good thing Luke could take it just as well as he could dish it out.

"A nobody like me!" He laughed. "And I suppose you think you're . . . who, exactly? Kate Middleton?"

"Kate Middleton is a social-climbing puppet if you ask me." She crossed her arms. "Do you realize I've been building my life from scratch ever since my parents cut me off? And since then, I've been able to rise up to partner at—"

"New York's second-largest hedge fund. I know."

"Meanwhile, you're stuck in your childhood town, building furniture for a living. You're one to judge."

"Oh, I love our friendly banter." Luke grinned, almost flirtatiously. "And I'll have you know carpentry is a very respectable art form." He smirked. "Too intricate for a snob like you to ever appreciate."

Why was this happening? she wondered. Why did every word he spoke fluster her more and more, while nothing she said seemed to affect him whatsoever?

"My God, are we finished here?" She groaned, finishing off the last of her bourbon.

"You really are in such a hurry to get away from me."

"Yes. I am. I want to go see my mom and, as you already know, I don't like you."

She let her head fall back in frustration. Instantly, she wished she hadn't. There, on the ceiling above them, was a sprig of mistletoe. She snapped her head back to face him, hoping he hadn't noticed what she had seen. But it was too late; he had seen it too.

"Well, would you look at that?" He shoved his one free hand into the pocket of his jeans and tried to avoid eye contact.

"I uh . . ." she stammered. "I should go upstairs. I think I've done all the socializing I need to do for the night. Or my whole lifetime."

"Okay," he agreed. "Sounds like a plan."

The two stood there for a moment, eyeing each other somewhat suspiciously.

"Okay then." She shrugged. "See ya around." She wanted to walk away but felt glued to the spot. Somehow she couldn't bring herself to move.

"Maybe just for the sake of tradition?" he blurted, gesturing at the mistletoe.

"I mean . . ." She blushed a little. "It *is* tradition."

Did I really just say that? She couldn't believe it. *Am I honestly going to let Luke Bennet kiss me? Wait. Do I actually* want *him to kiss me?* In that moment, she couldn't deny it. In the middle of this mess of a party, all she wanted was for the adrenaline to keep rushing.

He nodded with pursed lips. Then leaned in and gave her a quick peck on the lips. Darcy felt a surge of tingles race down from her head to her toes. From the look in his eyes, he felt it too.

"Wha—" he began.

"Don't say anything," she whispered, setting her glass down on the nearest ledge and taking his face in her hands. Before she knew it, they were kissing passionately, the sound of her heartbeat so loud in her own ears that it blocked out the music and the mindless chatter. *What are you doing, what are you doing?* her thoughts demanded of her. But she had no answer, and even though she tried, she couldn't stop kissing him. Why, after all, would she voluntarily break away from the best kiss she'd ever had?

"Ahem?" They were interrupted by the sound of somebody clearing his throat. Darcy peeled her face away from Luke's, snapping back to reality as if waking from a deep trance, humiliated to find that it was Carl Donovan standing before them now, one eyebrow raised and a smug smirk plastered across his face as if he were owed an explanation.

Carl Donovan was Darcy's on-again-off-again boyfriend who her father had wanted so badly for her to marry, all those years ago. Refusing to marry him was the reason she'd become more or less estranged from her dad since then.

What her dad didn't know—nor did anybody else, for that matter—was that ever since Carl had moved to New York City to practice law, he and Darcy had carried on with their on-and-off-again ways. Just because she didn't want to marry the guy didn't mean she didn't like him. What was so wrong about casually dating him when she felt like it, then taking her space when she felt like being alone? Wasn't that what every man wanted in a girl—someone independent, with no strings attached? The problem was that Carl wasn't like every man. He wanted something serious. He always had. This was his one major flaw, which sent Darcy running for the hills time and time again.

"Hey, Darce, whatcha doing?" he asked bitterly, but with a dose of optimism, as if she might jump in and say, "Wait! It's not what you think!"

"What does it look like I'm doing?" she replied.

"Uh . . ." This had him stumped.

"We're not together, Carl. I can do whatever I want."

"And *this* is what you want?" He gestured incredulously to Luke.

"Oh boy." Luke combed his hair back with one hand, then gave Darcy an awkward salute. "Have a good night, you two."

"Well, *that* was rude," she said to Carl, who himself was red with embarrassment and anger.

"*Me? I* was rude? You were making out with Luke Bennet in the middle of your family's Christmas party, for Christ's sake!"

"So?"

"*So?* It's been *two whole months* since you said you needed a week to think about us."

"What about us, Carl? There *is no us.*"

"Oh really." He cocked his head dramatically to the left. "So you mean to tell me I could walk out of here right now and you'd never see me again and that would be just fine with you? This is really it for us, huh? You're really okay with closing that door forever?"

Darcy was on the verge of confidently telling him that yes, it was over for good, but something held her back. Something in the familiar way his hands trembled when he was angry. She bit her lip, the memory of Luke's kiss still lingering.

"No," she gave in, feeling worn down. "No, fine. Can we get coffee tomorrow and talk? I'm really tired and, to be honest, I've had a lot to drink. I need to sleep."

"Oh." He face softened and relaxed. "Yes, yes, of course. Do you need help getting upstairs?"

"You wish," she said with a playful, lazy smile. "I'll see you tomorrow."

"I'm staying at the Glidden House." His smile was a hopeful one. "Coffee in the lounge at noon?"

"Sure. You got it," she said, and drifted up the stairs, delighted to be closing the door on this stranger-than-fiction night.

6

Darcy sat in the Glidden House lounge watching the winter day-light filter in through paned glass windows. She squinted against the light, resentful of its brightness. Why had she had to drink *quite* so much? She was not a big girl, and the truth was that three strong drinks acted on her system like seven.

But of course you overdid it, she reminded herself. The night was just one long strand of bizarre encounters, each one more uncomfortable than the one that came before it. She wondered what had become of Bingley and Jim Bennet. And what about Luke? Oh God, Luke. What had happened there? *Alcohol,* she told herself. *It* had *to be the alcohol.*

"Sorry to keep you waiting," Carl apologized, sliding into the chair across from her at exactly 12:03 p.m., just three minutes after their planned meeting time. In no way had he kept her waiting. In fact, she could have used a few more minutes to sit alone, gathering up her shattered memories from the night before.

"Not at all," she said feebly.

If Chris Mayfair was catalog handsome and Bingley Charles was movie star handsome and Luke Bennet was real-life-person handsome, then Carl Donovan was simply nice-looking. He had dark brown hair and neutrally gray eyes, a crooked nose that he got from a wayward golf ball at the age of nine, and a jaw that didn't do a good enough job accentuating itself, in Darcy's opinion. Today he was wearing a Burberry coat and red cashmere scarf, which he unwound from his neck and draped over the back of his chair as he sat.

"You look tired," he said.

"I am. I'm exhausted."

"So. What did you want to talk about?"

"Me? It seemed like you were the one with a lot on your mind, Carl."

"Fine, then I'll just jump right into it." He paused, folding his hands on the white tablecloth.

"You know what?" she interrupted, gesturing toward the nearest waiter. "We should get coffee. Excuse me!"

"How can I help you, miss?" the waiter asked.

"I'd like a double espresso, please," she said. "Carl?"

"I'll have a latte."

"Perfect." The waiter jotted down the orders. "Anything to eat?"

"Just the drinks for now, thanks." Darcy gave him her sweetest, kindest, most polite *now leave us alone, please* smile.

"So, like I was saying," Carl continued, "I'm tired of this

back-and-forth thing we've been doing. We get together, have an amazing month, and then you cut it off, for no other reason than that you're scared."

Scared? Ouch. He knew which words to choose to get her attention. Darcy Fitzwilliam wasn't scared of anything, and even though she knew he said it to be provocative, she resented the accusation.

"Scared? What am I scared of, exactly?"

"I don't know . . . love? Marriage? Commitment?"

"What are you talking about?" she joked. "Those are my three favorite words."

"I'm serious, Darcy. I want a change."

"So find someone new. Someone who wants all those things."

"But I don't want somebody new." His voice got serious and breathy. She hated when it did that. "I want you. And you want to be with me, too—at least some part of you must, otherwise you wouldn't keep coming back to me time and time again."

He did sort of have a point. She didn't *not* want to be with him. When they'd first met, during sophomore year of high school, he stood out as one of the most intelligent and driven people she'd ever met. He had read all the books she loved, and they would stay up late in the attic of his parents' house (when each of them was supposedly studying at the library) reading favorite lines to each other and arguing over the author's intended symbolism, and in time the arguing would turn to kissing, and before she knew it she'd be at her parents' breakfast table trying to explain how she could have possibly fallen asleep at the library *again*.

But then there had been the thing with Katie Smith during junior year. Katie was a sophomore with long blond hair who wore a lot of too-pink lip gloss. One weekend, while her parents were out of town, Katie decided to throw a huge party. One of those "everyone is invited" kind of deals. Darcy had a big chemistry exam to study for, and she had never been one for parties anyway, so she stayed home. Carl had not. When the party was over, Carl had showed up at Darcy's window, drunk beyond recognition and begging to be let in. She had let him in, only because she worried that his wailing was sure to attract the police. Once safely inside her bedroom, he said "I love you" for the first time, then passed out on the floor.

On Monday at school there were whispers in the hallway as she walked by. Everybody she passed avoided eye contact, as if they all had some big collective secret. Katie Smith herself seemed to be watching Darcy all through fourth period English.

"Why is everybody staring at me, Carl?" She pulled him over between fourth and fifth periods, grabbing him by the long sleeve of his Polo shirt. He turned white as a ghost.

"Babe, we have to talk."

"Really? You *think*? What the hell is going on?"

"As you know, I got really . . . *really* drunk on Saturday. I don't even remember how it happened, but somehow I ended up in Katie's bed and—"

"You slept with her," she said, stone cold, very matter of fact.

"Yes. But Darcy, I swear to God—"

"That's fine."

"What? It's not fine; it's terrible. Darcy, I never meant to hurt you in any way. I hope you'll find a way to forgive me."

"I do forgive you." She had laughed shallowly. "People make mistakes."

"Wait, are you serious?"

"Yeah," she had said, and meant it. "Nobody's perfect."

"Jesus, Darcy, you're incredible." He had stared bug-eyed in disbelief.

"Sure." She had shrugged. "Hey, listen, the bell is gonna ring any second. We should get back to class."

"Okay." He had beamed incredulously. "I'll see you after school."

"Sure," she had said dispassionately. He leaned in for a kiss but she turned her head so that he got her cheek instead, then she turned and hurried to class, holding her chin high above all the childishly curious eyes.

It wasn't that she had been lying when she said she forgave him. She had meant what she said. People make mistakes. Nobody is perfect. It wasn't that she was mad. The thing was, in that moment in the hallway, when he had confessed, the spark she had for him had just sort of gone out. She wasn't mad and she didn't hate him, she just didn't quite feel anything for him anymore.

She'd broken up with him a week later, out of boredom and apathy, but had taken him back a month after that, out of boredom and apathy as well. He worshipped her, and treated her like royalty to get her back. He sent flowers to her house almost every day, and wrote an awkward, boyish love song that he played for her clumsily on his uncle's antiquated acoustic guitar. It was cute, she thought. She was perfectly happy keeping him around as a constant ego booster, and they still got along pretty well. They laughed at all the same jokes and loved all the same books. They still shared political opinions and hated all the same classmates. And, of course, there was the fact that her parents adored him. As long as she was dating Carl Donovan of the Donovan family, they pretty much let her get away with anything she wanted. And so, because of all these things, she was perfectly content carrying on a romantic relationship with someone she wasn't in love with.

But then her father had decided the two should get married, and the rest was history.

"Now just isn't the time, Carl," she told him then, sitting across from his eagerly waiting puppy dog eyes. "My mom is really weak and I need to focus on being there for her. I can't commit to something I'm just not ready for."

"I have to be frank with you, Darcy. This is the last time I'm going to ask for you back. I'm thirty and I don't want to waste any more time. I want to get serious, start a family. And if you don't want it to be with you, then I'm going to have to move on."

"So . . . this is an ultimatum?"

"Yes. You have until Christmas to decide. If you want to be with me, really be with me, I need to know by then."

7

Darcy hung back in the Glidden House lobby while Carl excused himself and retreated to his suite. She turned her phone on and saw that it was glowing with texts and missed calls and voice mails from Millie back at the New York office. *Oh God,* she thought. *What fire do I need to put out now?* But she quickly realized there'd be nothing like a high-stress work call to take her mind off the tediously unpleasant events of the past few days.

"Millie, talk to me," she said, stepping out onto the freezing-cold terrace.

Millie updated her on the status of a few deals that were in the works, as well as the Overlook merger that was about to go south. Darcy made a mental note to call the director at Overlook to find out what was going on, and looking in on the lobby from the terrace, Darcy saw Bingley talking to the woman at the front desk.

"Hold on, Millie," she cut in. "I'm going to have to call you back." She hung up and hurried back into the lobby, eager to catch up with her friend on their respective nights. But he wasn't alone.

"Hey, Darcy," Jim said warmly, arm linked in Bingley's. "What are you doing here?"

Bingley saw her then and blushed.

"I was just getting coffee with Carl Donovan," she said in a singsong voice. "What are you two doing here, pray tell?"

"Do *not* judge me." Bingley playfully pointed a finger at her.

"Yes, yes." Jim rolled his eyes. "Bingley spent the night in my room, now could we please be adults about it and shut down the schoolgirl tittering? This is how rumors get started."

"Okay, okay." Darcy held up her hands in surrender. "You won't hear another word from me. I *am* technically the matchmaker here, so of course I reserve rights to take credit for this."

"Yes, fine," Bingley agreed. "Darcy Fitzwilliam Superstar."

"That's me."

"Carl wasn't trying to put a ring on it again, was he?" Jim asked sympathetically.

"Not quite. But something like that."

"What did you tell him?" Bingley asked.

"I don't know," Darcy sighed. "That I'd think about it. Meanwhile I have all this stuff I'm missing at work. I'm starting to think I should just go back. I don't want the place to fall apart without me there. Or worse, be just fine without me there."

"No!" Bingley protested. "You just got here!"

"I know, but—"

"Stay. Jim invited me to go caroling with him and his family tonight. You should come. She should, right, Jim?"

"Absolutely. It will be a blast. My mom has a secret hot chocolate recipe. You'll love it."

"I have a conference call, but I'll try to get out of it," she told them.

"Be there or be square, doll," Bingley said, ruffling her hair lovingly.

In her bedroom, Darcy fidgeted with a lampshade in the corner. It was on crooked, and no matter how she adjusted it, it slid right back into crookedness as soon as she moved her hands away. Of course, it wasn't really the lampshade that was on her mind. It wasn't the stress of work that was on her mind either, or the pressure of Carl's ultimatum. It wasn't even her mother's bad health. It was Luke.

What had that kiss been about? She had been drunk, yes, but not *that* drunk. She worried that it was something else, and that the alcohol was only partly to blame. She had a sick feeling in the pit of her stomach that perhaps the alcohol had only brought something to the surface that had been dormant within her for a long time. She only knew one thing for sure: nobody, no *thing*, had ever made her feel this way. Until now.

She got dressed in a pair of woolen, slim-fit pants and a burnt-umber cashmere sweater, then wrapped it all together beneath her favorite black Prada peacoat.

The Bennet house was only two blocks away, so she walked there on her own. It was arguably one of the smallest houses in the neighborhood, only two stories tall, built in a classic Tudor style. She walked up the cracked pavement of the driveway, trying to remember the last time she had been there, but she couldn't.

"Darcy! You made it!" Bingley cheered, pulling her in close.

"I told you she would." Jim appeared behind him. "Darcy has never been able to say no to hot chocolate and caroling." There was something in his tone of voice that suggested he was talking about something different altogether. That he was teasing her about something only the two of them would know. Or was she imagining it?

"Hey, Jim, where are the—" Luke bounded merrily into the room but stopped short when he saw Darcy standing there.

"Hey, Luke," she said shyly, trying not to redden.

"Hey, Darcy." He avoided eye contact, but tried to make his voice as friendly as possible. "Didn't know you'd be here." She saw him try to hold a determined smile back from taking over his mouth.

"Jim invited me."

"Cool, cool. So, uh . . . where's Carl?"

"No idea."

"Got it. Did you tell him about—"

"Don't!" she pleaded. "Let's not relive it."

"You say that as if it were a bad thing."

"It was a mistake. A drunken mistake."

"Interesting." He smirked. "The Darcy I remember *never* makes mistakes."

"Well, there's a first time for everything."

"I guess you're not as perfect as you like to pretend you are."

"And I guess you're not as much of a gentleman as you like to pretend to be."

"You're a fun girl, you know that?"

"What are you *talking* about?" She balked. Just then, two high school–age boys trudged down the stairs, drawing attention to themselves with their awkward gracelessness.

"Kit! Lyle!" Jim called out, once he saw them coming down the stairs. "So good of you to join us!"

Kit and Lyle grumbled something unintelligible.

"Who are these people?" Darcy asked Luke.

"These people? They're my brothers."

"Aren't your brothers like . . . five years old?"

"Um . . . they *were* five years old, once upon a time. See, people tend to . . . grow up over the years, you know, get older, et cetera. Are you really that self-absorbed?"

Darcy rolled her eyes and pretended not to hear him. Up close, she could see that Kit and Lyle were twins, each with ginger orange hair and a face full of freckles. One wore a black T-shirt with the word THRASHER written in jagged yellow letters, and the other wore a gray T-shirt with block letters that read SKATE, EAT, SLEEP, REPEAT.

Great fashion sense. Darcy mocked them in her own mind, then scolded herself for doing so. *They're kids, Darcy. They don't know any better.*

"Hey." Jim laughed at them as they approached. "Caroling attire, remember?"

"There's no such thing," Black Shirt said.

"Of course there is," Jim argued. "It's a tradition that's centuries old."

"Sorry," said Gray Shirt. "My bonnet is at the bonnet repair shop."

"Good one." Black Shirt approved of his brother's joke. Both boys snickered, amused with themselves.

"Ah, to be young again," Bingley fake-swooned.

"Which is Kit and which is Lyle?" Darcy asked, feeling annoyed that up until this point she was being made to guess.

"I'm Kit," said the one in the black shirt with yellow letters.

"Lyle," said the one in the gray shirt with white letters.

"Nice to meet you," she said, extending her hand. "I'm Darcy."

The two boys blinked dumbly. When she realized neither boy was going to shake her hand, she returned it back to her pocket.

"*Kit,*" Jim scolded. "*Lyle.* Don't be rude."

"Oh, leave 'em be," said Luke. "You remember what it was like to be fourteen. They'd literally rather be anywhere else than here."

"Fact," said Lyle.

"I'd rather be skating," said Kit.

"Hey," said Lyle, "don't you have a shirt that says that?"

"Yeah."

"You should have worn it."

"I know, yeah." Kit burped and they both laughed.

"Lovely." Darcy repressed her gag reflex.

She glanced over at Luke and saw that the expression on his face was one she hadn't seen on him before. It was a look of mildly pained discomfort, as if he were embarrassed by his baby brothers and the way they had presented themselves in front of Darcy. It was odd, because for as long as she could remember, Luke had been constantly above embarrassment or any other kind of societal influence. He had never been one to care what people thought, and he had prided himself on this characteristic. Though they'd butted heads throughout junior high and high school, Luke and Darcy had this in common. The thing was, he had always accused her of being a fake, of actually caring a great deal what people thought of her, despite what she said. Now she was beginning to wonder if this had been an instance of the pot calling the kettle black.

They took to the street as a group: Jim and Bingley and Luke and Kit and Lyle and Darcy. Had she known the caroling brigade would be so intimate she would have stayed home. With Bingley so obviously paired with Jim, and Kit and Lyle so obviously paired together, Darcy was left with Luke, walking tensely at his side. The night was getting increasingly cold, and she would have appreciated somebody to snuggle into, the way lucky Bingley had Jim. But things between her and Luke felt stranger than ever before, icier than ever before, and so she kept as much distance from him as possible, which, because of the wolf pack nature of their traveling bunch, was no more than a foot.

"Okay, let's do this one," Jim said, stopping outside a modest-sized house at the end of the block.

"But all their lights are off," Darcy pointed out.

"Exactly," said Jim. "That means no carolers have come by yet."

"Or it means they don't *want* any carolers."

"Nobody doesn't want carolers." Jim laughed at the thought.

"Oh boy." Darcy inhaled sharply. "Well go ahead. By all means, don't let me stop you." She gestured up the front walkway. Jim and Bingley trudged ahead.

"After you, madam," Luke said mockingly. She turned her nose up at him and power walked up the stairs.

Jim rang the doorbell and soon the house flickered awake, one window at a time. The door opened and there stood an elderly man and his wife, both in pin-striped pajamas. Jim sang a note to get the rest of the group on key.

"Oh look!" said the wife. "They're carolers, darling!" The man nodded happily to his wife as the gang began to sing, following Jim's lead.

"On the first day of Christmas, my true love sent to me: a partridge in a pear tree."

This is the song we're going with? Darcy inwardly groaned, but then made herself shake off the negativity, once she saw how delighted it was making the graying couple at the door.

"On the second day of Christmas, my true love sent to me: two turtle doves and a partridge in a pear tree."

And on they went, singing each verse, listing the three French hens and the four calling birds and the five golden rings and the six geese a-laying and the seven swans a-swimming and the eight maids a-milking and the nine ladies dancing and the ten lords a-leaping and the eleven pipers piping and the twelve drummers drumming. Darcy had so many questions about this song. First of all, who wrote it? Was the narrator male or female? And who was this wealthy-as-God true love? Who could possibly afford to send exotic animals and actual droves of human beings to somebody's house?

And if I were to have these ludicrous displays of wealth and affection delivered to me, would I be impressed or just horrified? Maids a-milking? As in women who are milking cows? Why would I want to see one person doing that, let alone eight all at once?

Who were these lords and why were they a-leaping, and how on earth could you work out the physical logistics of sending them all to somebody's home? And wasn't this slave labor of some kind? Surely the leaping lords and the milking maids and the piping pipers and the drumming drummers weren't getting paid for all this, were they? And what about the nine ladies dancing? What kind of dancing was this exactly, and was Darcy right to assume it was of a somewhat risqué nature? Did all of these performers and servants want to be there? Did they have families they'd rather be with? And what about the animals? Surely there were animal rights laws in violation. But then again, this song was from the year 1780, so it was safe to assume there were no animal rights laws to violate.

"That was so lovely." The woman clapped her hands together and turned to her husband. "Don't you think so, dear?"

"Absolutely," he agreed. "Won't you come in for some hot chocolate?"

"We'd love to," Jim decided for the group, ushering them in.

"Seems kind of rude to just . . . barge on in like this," Darcy mumbled under her breath.

"We're not barging in," Luke said. "He *invited* us in."

"He was just saying it to be polite."

"It's tradition, Darcy, and you know that. Carolers go from door to door and then get invited in for hot chocolate and treats. It's just how it works."

"Sure, but they didn't have their lights on. They didn't *want* carolers."

"They said our caroling was *lovely*."

"Again, they were just being polite."

"Oh yeah?" Luke smirked proudly as they entered the foyer to find a table generously piled with drinks and Christmas cookies.

"Whatever." Darcy crossed her arms, pretending not to be bothered that she'd lost this argument. She'd get him next time.

"Sick cookies!" Lyle said, diving for the five-pointed stars decorated with gold metallic-looking beads of sugar.

The night went on like this, the group shuffling from house to house singing "Twelve Days of Christmas" or "Hark! The Herald Angels Sing" or "Joy to the World" or any one they could remember clearly after the fourth house, once the numbing combination of cold and spiked eggnog was getting to their heads.

"Okay, where to now?" Bingley asked as they finished up at the Cole household on Merithew Street.

"It's almost midnight," said Darcy. "I think we're done."

"I know," Luke said with a mischievous smile. "Let's hit up the Fitzwilliam house."

"Ooh, good idea!" Bingley cheered. "They have the best eggnog in town."

"My mother is sick," she reminded them. "Now isn't the time."

"Oh, I don't know about that," said Luke. "I think now she could use some Christmas cheer more than ever."

Darcy glared at him.

"You know what? Fine." She gave in. "You're probably right."

She did not think he was right. In fact, she knew her mom was most likely asleep and her dad would come to the door, annoyed. But this would be a success for her personally for three reasons: (1) It would prove her right, thus giving her one win over Luke. (2) It would annoy her dad, thus getting back at him for his petty attitude toward her over the past eight years. And (3) she'd get to crawl into bed and abandon the awkwardness of the caroling gang once and for all.

Unfortunately for her, none of it went according to plan.

Her dad opened the door, surprised and delighted to see them there.

"We've had so many strangers come by tonight," he said. "I've been wondering when we'd get some familiar faces. And my own daughter nonetheless!" He pulled her in for an enthusiastic kiss on the cheek. His breath was redolent of eggnog. Ah, that explained it: he was drunk. Luke gave her his classic victory glance.

Okay yes, this, she thought, *this is exactly why you cannot fall for this guy. He's always going to have to have the last word, he's always going to have to win. It won't work. Please, dear Lord, spare yourself the grief.*

"Mrs. Fitzwilliam is asleep, but please come in and have some eggnog. We have so much of it left over you could fill a swimming pool, honest to God."

Darcy pushed her way through the doorway and poured herself a mug of eggnog, using a long silver ladle. It was her fifth one of the night. She took a generous gulp.

"Hey," Luke said with a hint of flirtation in his voice. "Looks like you're standing under mistletoe . . . again."

"Goddammit," Darcy cursed. "What is with my family and mistletoe? Hang it up in one place, sure, but all over the house? I mean, this is just excessive. Good thing this time I'm under it alone."

"Not anymore," Luke said, sliding up next to her so that they were both, once again, standing together under mistletoe.

Wait a second, she thought, *is he still thinking about me too? What does he want from me? Do we*—she grimaced inwardly—*have feelings for each other?*

"You are *so* childish," Darcy scoffed, turning away from him. But before she could stop herself, before she knew what she was doing, she spun back around, pulled him in by the collar, and kissed him on the mouth.

8

The light pierced through blue gingham curtains, jolting Darcy awake. Her head throbbed with the aftermath of too much eggnog. *Where am I?* she thought, in a disoriented panic. She blinked and looked around, settling back into reality, and realized that she was in her childhood bedroom. In her underwear. *Weird*, she thought. *Where are my pajamas?* She glanced to her left and saw, to her absolute horror, that Luke Bennet was in her bed, fast asleep.

Mother—! She had to bite her tongue to keep from screaming out. *Why, Darcy, why?* Very slowly, she sat up and removed the covers from her body, then tiptoed to her bathroom door, where her fleece bathrobe hung on a hook, as quietly as possible, so as to not wake him. She didn't know exactly what her plan was from here on out. Maybe she'd hide out in the downstairs library until she could be sure that he was gone. Or maybe now was as good a time as any to fly back to New York and pretend none of this had ever happened.

"Morning, angel." She spun around to see Luke sitting up in bed, stretching his arms in each direction. Dammit, she hadn't moved fast enough.

"Uh . . ." She laughed nervously. "What did you just call me?"

"Angel. It's what you told me to call you, don't you remember? Right after we confessed our true love for each other? It would be a shame if you don't remember that; it was seriously magical. Best night of my life. Hands down."

Darcy's heart plummeted. For a second she thought she might throw up. What had she done? How could she have possibly said those things to him? And now he loved her? In the span of one drunken night she had managed to get herself in way over her head. Her whole body surged with regret and remorse.

Just then, Luke started laughing.

"Oh my God." He gasped for breath. "The look on your face."

"What?" she demanded. "What is so funny?"

"I'm just kidding, Darcy. Nothing happened between us last night."

"Oh thank God." She clutched her chest. "Are you sure? You're sure nothing happened?"

"Yes. You were really drunk and you kissed me downstairs. We were making out and you brought me up to your bedroom and started taking off your clothes—"

"Ugh," Darcy cringed. "That's bad."

"Oh no, it was good. It was all very good, until you flung yourself onto the bed and passed out. Literally. You were out cold."

"Well, that's embarrassing, but it's less embarrassing than if I had actually slept with you, so I'll take it."

"Well, you did want to sleep with me, you made that much clear."

"I did not."

"Then how'd we get up here?"

"I don't know, Luke, I was wasted. For all I know you tried to take advantage of me and brought me up here just because you wanted to." *Don't let this become a thing,* she repeated. *Don't let this become a thing.*

But she knew this much was true: she did remember kissing him first, and had a blurry memory of leading him seductively up the stairs.

"If I had wanted to take advantage of you, I would have. You gave me plenty of opportunities for that. But I'm a gentleman. And sex with a girl who is that drunk can't possibly be consensual."

"Well, good for you, Mr. Morality."

"So, breakfast time?"

"No!" she laughed, appalled at the suggestion. "It's time for you to go home. I have calls to make."

"To all your girlfriends, telling them about the hottie you woke up next to this morning?"

"Um, definitely not. For your information, if I don't have time for boyfriends I definitely don't have time for girlfriends. I have colleagues and employees, all of whom are depending on me to make this investment deal go through."

"That's depressing."

"Maybe to you."

"It's not depressing to you that you don't have friends or a boyfriend?"

"Definitely not," she snapped. "I follow my passions and dreams every day and live a very rewarding life because of it."

"And . . . hedge funds are your passion?"

"Money is my passion. Making money is my passion."

"Cold, hard cash, huh?"

"Mm-hm."

"Sounds . . . fulfilling."

"Okay, buddy, time for you and your judgment to leave. Great chattin' with ya."

"Okay, okay," he gave in, standing up. Darcy was profoundly relieved to see that he was wearing his jeans from the night before. "I'm leaving."

"Okay then." She crossed her arms when he tried to give her a hug. Alternately, she extended her hand for a handshake, which he gave her amusedly.

"You're a real . . . interesting girl, Darcy."

"Wow, fun and interesting? I'll take that as a compliment."

"Good," he said. "You should."

She gave a half smile and closed the door behind him.

What was all that about? she wondered. If he bothered her so much when she was sober, why did she suddenly feel so drawn to him when drunk? And if she disliked him so intensely, then why did she feel an odd sense of disappointment creeping up inside her now that he had left? And he didn't have feelings for her, did he? The way he was talking, it was starting to seem like perhaps he might. Or was it all in her head? And why did it matter? Why did she care? *I don't have feelings for Luke Bennet,* she told herself. *There's just no way. Right? I mean, maybe if he were more . . .* She shook her head, cutting the thought off at its root.

She had an hour until her conference call, and she decided to nap until then. She could think of nothing better in this moment than to be unconscious, free from the confusing buzz that was currently disrupting her mind. She took off her bathrobe and slipped back under the covers. The pillows, to her dismay, now smelled like Luke.

"Ugh-h-h," she groaned, trying to summon the energy to get new pillowcases from the cabinet in the hallway. But suddenly the effort didn't seem worth it. Suddenly, she found that she didn't even want to get rid of the smell. She nuzzled her face into the fabric, breathed in deeply, and was asleep.

She woke an hour later to the jarring sound of her phone buzzing violently against the wooden nightstand. It was Millie.

She snapped herself awake and spoke into the receiver. "This is Darcy. Whattaya got for me?"

"The deal fell through." Millie's voice was timid.

"*What?*" Darcy nearly fainted.

9

It was an hour later when Bingley came over, carrying a box of gourmet chocolates under one arm.

"Let's eat them out by the pool," Darcy suggested grumpily. "The sun seems to have come out for a second. We might as well soak it up."

They each took their own lounge chair and stretched out across the blue canvas.

"You're going to be okay, Darcy. It's not like they're going to fire you over this, are they?"

"No," she grumbled. "We were just hoping to make a lot on this one. I was going to finally buy my boat."

"Aw, poor baby! Maybe the boat will have to wait until next year."

"It's not just me, though." She tried to justify her disappointment so that he'd understand she wasn't really as much of a selfish bitch as she had just made herself seem. "I wanted this for our clients. I do this for them too, you know. It's one thing to make yourself rich, but it's another feeling altogether to make other people rich."

"That's a very . . . interesting version of humanitarianism."

"Shut up." She shoved him playfully. "I never claimed it was noble. If anything, it's probably some glitch in my psychology that makes me need to make droves of people happy constantly in order for my ego to be properly nourished."

"Hmm. Cool insight. At least you understand yourself."

"Maybe I shouldn't have come home," she sighed. "I was so scared when I heard about my mom that I hopped on the first plane that I could, but now it's like she doesn't even need me. And she says she's fine. But I don't know. Something tells me she's just putting on a brave face and that I should stay. At least until Christmas. I mean, people are mostly gone from the office anyway . . . Let's talk about something else, before I crawl into my bed and never leave."

"So what's the deal with you and Luke?" Bingley asked, biting into a chocolate.

"What do you mean?" she asked, trying not to sound too flustered. "There's no deal with me and Luke."

"You were *literally* all over each other last night after caroling. You *literally* took him up to your room."

"Wha—No, that's not—I . . . uh—"

"First of all, you are adorable when you stammer. Second of all, we all saw you. You don't need to be embarrassed. Luke's hot."

"Ugh," she groaned, and let her head hang down, resting it in her palms. "He's hot but he's the worst and I hate him. I can't believe people saw us kissing. What do my parents put in that eggnog? I mean, *good God*."

"You sound like a fifth grader. Getting all flustered over a boy. You *like* him."

"I do not."

"You're blushing."

"Okay, *fine*." She threw her hands up. "The truth is, I have no idea how I feel about him or what's going on. But if I'm being really honest with myself, I would say at this point it's safe to say I don't *not* like him."

"Ha! Knew it."

"All right, all right." She rolled her eyes and stuffed a chocolate into her mouth. "No gloating."

"So what's the problem? Just date him!"

"Bingley, I can't! He's a jerk! I mean, he means well, but all we do is push each other's buttons. And it's not like I'm going to leave New York, so there's just no point."

"Who said anything about leaving New York? What's wrong with a little winter vacation fling? I mean, why fight it?"

"I don't know . . ." she said. "To be honest I don't even want to think about it. Whatever happens will happen." But just as she said it, a theory began to form: What if she didn't want this fling to happen because she knew it could never be only a fling?

"Funny how much can happen in such a short time," Bingley remarked whimsically. "Just two days ago we hadn't seen each other in eight years, and now here we are, both making out with Bennet brothers. Love it."

"That's right!" Darcy's eyes lit up, remembering the exciting new romance between two of her favorite people. "How are things going with Jim? He's great, isn't he?"

"Oh my God, so great," Bingley gushed. "We've been weirdly inseparable ever since you introduced us. I don't think I've ever felt this way about anyone before."

"What are you going to do about what's-his-name?"

"You mean Marco?"

"If Marco is the man you live with in Los Angeles, then yes."

"Oh, we broke up months ago."

"I'm sorry. I didn't—"

"Yeah, yeah, whatever," he said, brushing it off. "But listen, I'm thinking of moving back here to be with Jim."

"*Excuse me?*" She gasped, almost choking on a chocolate.

"Yeah, what do you think?"

"I think it's *crazy.*"

"Whoa, don't hide how you *really* feel or anything."

"Well, you asked me! You have this awesome life in Los Angeles. I don't see why you'd want to give all that up to come back to *Pemberley.*" She couldn't help grimacing as she said it.

"Um, how about *true love?*"

"Okay, sure, maybe. But look, you just met this guy, Bingley. Like, *just.* Maybe you should take a little more time to get to know him. Slowing things down just a tad never hurt anybody, right?"

"Maybe you're right."

"I know things are exciting with him right now; you're in the honeymoon stage of the honeymoon stage, babe. But try to think about this practically."

"Practically how?"

"Don't get me wrong. I adore Jim. But he's not like us. He

doesn't care about the excitement and the drive of the big cities. We dream big, Bingley. That's why we aren't here anymore."

"Okay, that's a good point."

"*Thank you.*"

"I have a date with him tonight. Do you think I should cancel?"

"I'm not saying you should blow him off forever. I'm just saying you should take a little bit of space to get some perspective. You've been spending every day with him since you got to Pemberley. Any healthy relationship needs some breathing room."

"All right. Please note that I'm not doing this because I think you're any sort of oracle on what a healthy relationship is"—he rolled his eyes as if to say, *Because you certainly are not*—"but because I think you happen to be right on this one point."

"Noted."

Bingley took out his phone and dialed.

"You have his number memorized?" Darcy gawked. "How is that even possible? You've been with him twenty-four seven. When did you have time to—"

"The heart wants what it wants, okay? Now shh."

Darcy made a zipping motion across her lips.

"Hey babe!" Bingley lit up as he spoke into the phone. "Hey, so I'm feeling a little bit under the weather and I think I should probably stay in and rest up tonight. . . . Ugh, I know. Exactly." He giggled. "I can't even remember the last time I slept." Darcy stuck her tongue out in feigned disgust. "Okay, so talk tomorrow? . . . Awesome. . . . Love ya, too!"

"You're already saying *I love you*?" Darcy couldn't believe it. She'd never said those words to anyone, let alone someone she'd only just met.

"Not *I love you*. Just *Love ya*. There's a difference."

"Sure. Okay." She squinted suspiciously.

"Oh, Darcy, I already miss him so much."

"Oh my God, you are such a girl."

"I take that as a compliment."

"Let's get out of here." Darcy yawned, stretching her arms above her head. "I need to get my mind off things. Let's go dancing."

"Dancing? Wow, girl. I like the way you think. But it's barely five o'clock. Nowhere will be open."

"Club Avon opens at seven. By the time we're done dolling ourselves up it will be perfect timing."

"Alrighty then." He popped a chocolate in his mouth and chewed. "Let's do it."

The two retreated to Darcy's room and Darcy had Lorna bring up the spare rack of outfits and accessories that they kept stored in the east wing study that was otherwise mostly unoccupied. They turned on Darcy's old CD player and blasted David Bowie from the speakers. They draped silvery scarves around each other's necks and modeled an array of pretentious hats, strutting and posing to the music.

"Ooh, this shirt will look amazing on you." Darcy picked out a neon-pink, deep-V, long-sleeved T-shirt made of some sort of silk blend.

"Jesus Christ, where did this stuff come from?"

"I don't really know." She shrugged, thinking about it for the first time. "We've always just sort of had it."

"Do you think your dad had a secret life as a gay disco aficionado? Because that's what it seems like."

"Have you *met* my dad?"

"Or maybe it was both of your parents! Maybe they were these major party animals and had these totally different personalities than the ones we know."

"My parents are both seriously square. Dream on."

"Well, *excuse me* for trying to exercise my imagination."

"You're excused. Trust me, if either of my parents had a wild bone in their bodies they might have been more sympathetic to me not wanting to marry Carl." She wrinkled her nose when she said his name. "But no such luck."

"You never know," he said, playing devil's advocate. "What if that's precisely why they were so hard on you about it? Because it reminded them of their rebellious days."

"Hmm," she said, shimmying into a black velvet cocktail dress. "That theory is realistic enough. Here, can you zip me up?"

He pulled the black zipper up along her spine.

"How do I look?" she asked.

"Gorgeous," he replied. "What about me?"

She looked him up and down. He was wearing a white-collared shirt underneath a coal-colored vest, with a plaid cashmere scarf around his neck.

"Dashing," she declared. "Let's blow this pop stand."

"You got it, doll face."

The first setback in their plan to dance their troubles away came when the Avon Club was closed for filming.

"Filming?" Darcy scoffed. "Who comes to film in Pemberley freaking Ohio?"

"Anyone. It's much cheaper than Hollywood. Can't you, like, pull some strings to get us in?"

"Pull strings?" She laughed. "First of all, they're filming; they're not letting anyone in. Second of all, who do you think I am?"

"Uh, I don't know. A very important person?"

"Well, thank you, that's very sweet, but sadly I have no pull whatsoever in Pemberley, Ohio. Here, I'm just another rich bitch."

"Fair enough." He gave in to the idea that they would not be dancing. "To the Tavern?" he asked.

"To the Tavern," she agreed.

And that is how they found themselves at the Starlight Tavern, drinking antisocially in the corner by a crackling fireplace. The Starlight Tavern was a local and beloved bar steeped in Ohio history Darcy had never bothered to learn about. You could tell by the tightly packed brick walls and the rusty brass beer taps that interesting characters from all walks of life had been drinking here, and that's all Darcy needed to know. She found it much more interesting to imagine the lives of the Starlight Tavern patrons than to actually know them. In her head, it was all very romantic.

"Oh boy, this Scotch is strong." Bingley's face puckered, trying to handle the intensity of the liquid.

"I know," she beamed warmly. "Isn't it incredible?" Back in New York she had become strict with herself and her drinking habits and never had more than two drinks a week. But this was vacation, and for better or for worse, she was going to act like it. She couldn't figure out what the hell this trip was for or about, but she was going to make the best of it.

"Sure . . . that's one word for it. Would it kill them to put a little soda in it or something? You know, so it doesn't taste like straight-up smoke?"

"No, no, that would just dilute it! Bingley, this is twenty-one-year-old Scotch. It's supposed to taste smoky. That's part of the beauty of it. The flavor is so pure, you can actually taste the wood that it was aged in."

"Yeah, you're not exactly convincing me, babe," he said, then almost choked on his Scotch. "Goddammit," he cursed, hiding his face.

"Don't be so dramatic." She rolled her eyes.

"No, it's not that," he whispered harshly. "It's *Jim*."

"What's Jim?" She didn't understand.

"*It's Jim*," he repeated. "He just walked in."

"So? Go say hi."

"I can't go say hi," he reminded her, panicking, "because you told me to tell him I wasn't feeling well and that I was going to stay in, *remember*?"

"Oh no." She put her arm on Bingley's shoulder, trying to calm him down. "Should we try to sneak out before he sees us?"

"*Bingley?*" It was too late; they had been spotted. Jim, who was apparently at the Tavern alone, approached them where they sat.

"Jim! Hey!" Bingley stood up to give him a hug, but Jim backed away.

"You said you weren't feeling well," Jim reminded him. "I

thought you were staying in and that's why you couldn't do dinner."

"I, uh . . ." he stammered. "I wasn't feeling well. But then Darcy needed to talk to me, so I rallied and, uh—" He cleared his throat and took a deep breath. "No, Jim, listen. The truth is I'm feeling fine. I only canceled because I was worried we're moving too fast and I didn't want you to think I've been coming on too strong."

"Oh." Jim seemed confused, maybe even slightly suspicious. "Or maybe it's that I'm coming on too strong for you."

"No!" Bingley protested. "It's not that at all! It was so stupid. I really just—"

"I wish you would have just told me." Now Jim looked hurt, maybe even somewhat repulsed. "It's weird that you would . . . lie about something like that for no reason."

"No, Jim, it's not like that. You don't understand. I—"

"You're right. I don't understand. But I think I'm gonna head out. I guess I'll be seeing you around." He shoved his hands into his pockets and turned to leave.

"Dammit." Bingley contorted his face at Darcy. "What have I done?"

"Oh my God." She took his hand. "This is all my fault. I am so sorry. Go after him. Tell him it was my fault."

"Couldn't you have said that when he was here a second ago?"

"Ugh, I know. I'm sorry. I froze," she apologized earnestly. "But go catch up to him! Go, run, it will be romantic. He'll love it, I promise."

"Like I'm ever listening to love advice from you again!"

"Fine, don't listen. Maybe I was right in the first place. Maybe this relationship really did need the brakes put on it and now is as good a time as any to find out that you're not meant to be."

"Screw that." He stood. "I'm going after him."

"That's my boy," she said, slapping his butt gently as he hurried after Jim.

They'll be fine, she told herself, now sitting alone. *That was nothing more than a minor setback. A lesson in Early Relationship Glitches 101.*

She worked on finishing her drink, figuring that once it was empty she'd head home early. Just then, the Tavern door swung open, and in with the cold came Luke Bennet. To Darcy's surprise, he was with somebody. Who was that? Darcy squinted through the dim lighting and saw that it was Charlotte Collins, a girl who had also gone to their high school. Darcy had always thought Charlotte was a spineless teacher's pet, and she had gotten on Darcy's nerves. Charlotte had interpreted Darcy's sexually awakened and enlightened ways as slutty, and didn't mind expressing these beliefs during a heated moment in debate class. Darcy knew from her recent encounter with Bingley and Jim that it was too late to pretend she wasn't there. They had seen her, and there was no way out of this one.

"Luke! Hi!" She waved them over with as much friendliness as she could possibly muster. "You literally just missed your brother."

Luke seemed to turn white upon seeing her.

"Ah, yes, we saw," he replied stiffly.

"You're Darcy Fitzwilliam, aren't you?" Charlotte asked with a plastic smile. "You went to high school with us."

"Sure did," replied Darcy.

"Oh, uh, sorry," Luke stammered. "Darcy, this is Charlotte. Charlotte, this is Darcy."

"We know each other, silly," Charlotte teased. "I mean *hello*, we just said that." She slapped his coated arm playfully, causing the diamond on her ring finger to twinkle in the dim Tavern light.

Oh my God, thought Darcy in a panic, *is he . . . engaged?*

"Wow!" Darcy sat back, composing herself. "That's a beautiful ring." In all honesty, Darcy did not like the ring. It was small and shapeless and unremarkable. But she had to say something.

"Thank you!" Charlotte beamed and gripped lovingly onto Luke's arm. "We're getting married on New Year's Day!"

Luke's forehead was starting to sweat. He smiled dumbly at his bride-to-be while avoiding eye contact with Darcy at all costs.

"Is that so?" Darcy asked. "Well, congratulations."

"We just decided," Luke blurted out awkwardly. "It wasn't planned or anything."

"He's so spontaneous," Charlotte gushed. "We've been dating forever, and then just one day, out of the blue, ta-da!" She held up her hand to show off the sliver of a ring once more.

"*So* spontaneous," Darcy agreed, trying to keep a straight face.

"I'm going to run to the little girls' room," Charlotte said politely. "Be back soon!"

Ugh, Darcy thought, *she totally is the kind of person to call it the "little girls' room." Creepy.*

"What the hell, Luke?" she hissed, once Charlotte was out of earshot.

Luke double-checked that she was really gone, then slid into the seat across from Darcy. "Darcy, I'm sorry. It's not what you think."

"Ha!" she laughed bitterly. "Are you not engaged to Charlotte Collins despite making out with me twice in the last forty-eight hours?"

"I am, but it's not like that."

"Like what?"

"I didn't cheat on her. I'm not a cheater."

"You have my attention," she said, lifting the glass to her lips.

"Charlotte and I have been dating for a long time," he explained hurriedly, "and recently our relationship sort of hit a plateau. So we decided to take a break. It was mutual. I thought it was the right thing to do. But then you came to town and you pointed out how my life isn't adding up to anything here in Pemberley. I've been doing a lot of thinking and I've realized that it's okay that my life doesn't look like anything from the outside. I'm a small-town guy, and it's time I own up to my life, which is here with Charlotte, who's always been there for me. It's time I commit to this life." By the time he was finished, Luke was panting, hands tapping anxiously against the tabletop.

"Well . . ." Darcy tried to smile. "I'm glad I was able to clear that up for you."

10

Later that night, Darcy sat at the foot of her childhood bed, staring into the white damask wall. No matter how hard she tried, she couldn't parse the feelings she was having. Her mind was a twisted-up labyrinth of questions, like *Why do I care if Luke is engaged? I know for a fact that he isn't right for me, right? I've never in my life questioned my feelings for Luke, so why would I now? Would I actually want to be with Luke? Why did I kiss him? Why did I kiss him twice? Why did he kiss me back both of those times? Does he feel anything for me? Does he actually want to be engaged to Charlotte Collins? Why should I even care if he wants to be engaged to Charlotte Collins; it's not as if I'd rather he be engaged to me, is it? Or, is it?*

No, she told herself, *I do not want to be with Luke. I am not*

the kind of girl who falls for a small-town carpenter with no ambi-
tion. I have big things ahead of me, and none of them include be-
ing married to someone as boorish as Luke Bennet in Pemberley
goddamn Ohio. These feelings for him are just the result of a tem-
porary moment of insanity caused by the disorientation of being
home to see my sick mom and the fear of Carl's stupid ultimatum.
Plus the alcohol; you can't forget about all the alcohol.

She stood up and brushed off her skirt, feeling better. Now
that she understood her feelings and the situation, she could
shake it off and move forward. Now that she had a grasp, she
could be proactive. Proactive step number one was brilliant, if
she did say so herself: get into bed and watch hours of mindless television until she forgot entirely about Luke and about
Carl and about the deals back in New York and the anxiety about
her mother's health, and even forgot her own name. She got on
her knees to pull her suitcase out from under the bed. Out with
the suitcase came a book bound in blue leather.

"Oh my God," she said out loud. "The Pemberley High yearbook!"

She held it in her hands for a moment but decided there was
nothing in it she needed to see, no reason to take a trip down
memory lane to the least favorite part of her life, and tossed it
onto the silk-upholstered reading nook. She slipped into her
nightgown and buried herself in bed, happy to find that Lorna
had exchanged all the Luke-smelling pillowcases for new ones.
She turned on the TV and put on her guiltiest of guilty pleasures:
Gilmore Girls. And no, not the new Netflix season, but the old
episodes, from the year 2000.

Ever since she was thirteen years old, this had been her safe place: in bed with the blankets pulled up to her chin, lights turned all the way off so that the only light came from the blue glow of *Gilmore Girls*. She had never, and would never, tell anybody about this ritual, or that she could tolerate such a saccharine, tediously dull show as *Gilmore Girls,* let alone adore it, let alone rely on it to maintain her sanity from time to time.

As the opening theme began to play and Carole King began to sing "If you're out on the road / Feeling lonely and so cold . . ." and the montage of Rory and Lorelai as the ultimate mother–daughter duo moved across the screen, Darcy felt a warm sense of calm roll over her, something she hadn't felt in years.

But the blue book was peeking out at her from the reading nook. She tried to ignore it, focusing on the witty quips of the episode's opening scene, but every few minutes her attention would be pulled back to the book. She wondered why she hadn't simply shoved it back under the bed, where it had come from. She could have done so easily, but instead she had thrown it into the nook, where it was glaringly visible. Why?

Don't be ridiculous, she told herself. *You're overthinking it. When this episode is over, I'll put it back under the bed where it belongs. End of story. Just watch your show. Watch how dependably adorable Rory is in her schoolgirl outfit and her naive good-girl bookworm routine that would be so painfully annoying on anyone else except her. Watch how charming that little fake town is with its little fake people who are so happy and safe in their daily routines, satisfied by the minutiae of life. Watch Rory's dependably adorable boyfriend fit in so nicely with her family, and his naive good-boy routine that would be so painfully annoying on anyone else except him.*

Of course, Darcy much preferred the episodes when Rory started dating bad boy Jess, instead. He really came in and shook things up. They had such a dysfunctional, forbidden, tense vibe going on between them. Darcy had always found that dynamic to be alluring. Jess had been so much more intriguing than boring Dean.

Against her will, Darcy glanced over at the yearbook again.

Okay, fine, she thought, *if you wanna read the dumb book, then just go read it. No use with this back-and-forth business.*

She paused the TV and reluctantly dragged herself out of bed. She curled up into the reading nook and opened the yearbook. She flipped through the glossy pages, with her eyes protectively squinted, the way you would while going through a haunted house. Her eyes roved over the rows of black-and-white square photos of classmates she'd mostly forgotten. People who mostly still probably lived right here in Pemberley. She saw Carl's stiff, slicked-back hair and laughed. He had always been so . . . normal. So wildly normal that it bordered on rebellious. How could anybody be *that* normal? Next to his picture he had written in green ink, "Darcy, you are the most incredible girl I've ever met. You're brave and adventurous, and every moment with you is a thrill. Wouldn't it be nice if we were older and we wouldn't have to wait so long to have the perfect life together we've always imagined? I love you. Love, Carl."

She cringed a little bit, remembering the nausea she had felt upon reading these words all those years ago. He had quoted the Beach Boys, for Christ's sake. On top of that, Darcy didn't view herself as any of those things, except maybe brave at times, and so this message to her only made her feel disconnected and cold, as if he didn't know her at all. And what was the "perfect life" she had always imagined? Wasn't it exactly what she had now, living in a posh loft-style apartment in Manhattan with a job to die for? If so, then why wasn't she happy?

As she flipped through the pages, she noticed that there wasn't a whole lot of writing on them. A few people she hadn't ever actually been friends with had signed their pictures with generic niceties like "Hey Darcy, you're awesome, never change!" and "Let's make sure to keep in touch!" and "Hope you have a great life!" She rolled her eyes as she looked them over; none of these people had kept in touch. And, of course, she hadn't bothered to keep in touch with them anyway. In fact, she could barely remember them even now, looking at their pixilated faces. Chris Mayfair had written over his face, "Darcy! Remember when you made Mr. Prescott cry in homeroom? That was hilarious. I'll never forget it, or you! Keep in touch always! Love, Chris."

Darcy rolled her eyes again. She couldn't remember what she had done or said to make Mr. Prescott cry, but she hated whenever anyone reminded her of her mean streak. She didn't like this part of herself, but it was a part of her nonetheless, and had been since childhood.

On the next page was a collage of black-and-white photos of the student body doing various activities. Performing in the school plays—everything from *Annie* to *A Midsummer Night's Dream* to *Peter Pan* to *Rent*—playing sports, winning championships, hanging out casually in the quad in between classes. She came across the pages of photos from the debate team and stopped. There was Luke in a suit and crooked tie, standing at a podium, deep in thought, buried in concentration. And, across the room, at the other podium, was Darcy herself, mouth open in a moment of determined arguing.

A flood of nostalgia rushed through her. The memories of hating Luke, of constantly wanting to prove him wrong, of going to any lengths to make sure he understood that he was inferior to her, all of it suddenly seemed so clear: she felt this way and did these things because secretly, deep down, she knew that Luke had it right all along. He took it easy, he appreciated things for the way they were, he knew what it was to be grateful, to feel satisfied, and, as a result, he was going to get to know happiness. She fought him tooth and nail because she was worried he had something she'd never have, and she wanted to prove him wrong for the sake of her own peace of mind. When she had been drunk she could see this clearly, that though he might seem simple, he actually carried with him the secret to easy living, to pure living, and that's why she had kissed him. Deep down, she had been secretly attracted to him all along.

This is the worst, she thought, slamming the book shut. *What the hell am I supposed to do with this information?*

She shoved the book back under the bed, pushing it deeper so that it didn't have any chance of getting out this time. She grabbed Little Lion off the shelf and got back into bed, aggressively curling him into the crook of her elbow for comfort and support. She pressed Play and fell asleep to the sounds of Rory Gilmore precociously discussing *Madame Bovary.*

She woke in the morning to an excited knock on her door.

"Who is it?" She yawned, disoriented and puffy-eyed.

"It's Lorna, dear! Your presence is requested in the dining room."

"Really? So early?"

"It's . . . ten, dear."

Darcy snapped her face toward the clock underneath the TV and saw that it was, in fact, ten in the morning. How had she slept so long? On the TV screen was a sign that read "ARE YOU STILL WATCHING GILMORE GIRLS? YES/NO."

"I'll be right there!" she told Lorna.

"As soon as you can, dear. Your parents have good news they're eager to tell you."

News? That's odd, thought Darcy. After all, neither of them had exactly gone out of their way to speak to her since she'd arrived in Pemberley. She hurried out of bed and sat in front of the vanity to put her best face on.

Darcy entered the dining room, bracing herself for the worst. Sure, Lorna had said that the news was good news, but that felt so unusual to her, it was hard to believe it wasn't just a hoax to get her downstairs with the whole family before springing something awful on her. The dining room was sparkling clean and decorated shamelessly in white lilies. Her whole family was there: Mom, Dad, and three brothers, all chatting joyously. She let her stiff shoulders relax a little bit, shimmying off the tension. Still, she wasn't used to seeing them all together like this—it had to have been at least a decade since all three of her brothers were in one place—so she approached with caution.

"Darcy!" her mother called cheerily from her wheelchair at

the head of the table. "Come join us." The color was back in her cheeks, Darcy was glad to see.

"Where were you at the Christmas party?" her middle brother, James, who was staying at his fiancée's family home for the winter, asked with a nagging tone Darcy did not appreciate. "I didn't see you all night."

"I know where she was," teased William, the youngest. "She was under the mistletoe making out with Luke Bennet."

Gasps rippled around the table. Darcy thought she might faint with embarrassment. She couldn't stand the thought that anyone had seen her acting out such base instincts, even though they were her family, who she'd become accustomed to disappointing.

"Is that true, Darcy?" her father asked, horrified.

"With all due respect . . ." She swallowed hard. "I don't think it's really anyone's business, is it?"

"Actually, it is somewhat my business," said Mr. Fitzwilliam, "because I just recently spoke with Andrew Donovan, who said things were quite serious again with you and Carl."

"Dear God." Darcy let out an exasperated sigh. "The way news travels in this town, I swear. Listen, Dad, things are not serious with Carl and me. In fact, we haven't even been dating in like over a year, so I'm sorry to burst that bubble again, but the status of Carl and Darcy is same as ever: not happening.

"Yes, it's true, maybe you heard, that he gave me an ultimatum and I have until Christmas to decide if I'm going to be with him, otherwise he's cutting me off for good." She rolled her eyes as she said this. "But I really don't see it going his way. Carl just doesn't . . . do it for me, okay? I don't know what else to say about it. So, as a grown woman, I think I have the right to make out underneath the mistletoe with anyone I please, thank you very much."

By the time she finished she was out of breath. *Wow,* she thought, *that train of thought really got away from me.* She had intended to shut the whole conversation down quickly and concisely; she had not intended for it to become a one-woman rant. Her family members blinked dumbly as a stiff silence permeated the room. Hadn't they all been laughing carelessly just a moment ago, before she had entered the room? Was there something about her that tended to end the fun so abruptly? Was she broken in some way? What was it about her that caused her to be the black cloud drifting over everybody else's good time?

"Why do we even care who Darcy marries?" Kenneth, her oldest brother, asked. "James is marrying an heiress to the largest chocolate company in America, I'm married to an *actual* Nobel Prize winner in medicine, and William is dating that Kellogg girl! I think we've got it covered. Darcy can be a spinster if she wants, and it does seem like that's what she wants."

"Thanks, Kenneth," Darcy snipped sarcastically.

"You're welcome," he replied, pretending to not hear the sarcasm. Mr. Fitzwilliam took this all in; it seemed to make him feel slightly better.

"Okay, okay," interrupted Mrs. Fitzwilliam. "All of this is getting unpleasant. And I called everyone here today to discuss good news. Good news only, people. So, let's start with William. He has an announcement. William?" She gestured to him excitedly. William Fitzwilliam sat slouched in his chair, not used to the attention on him.

"I, uh . . ." He chuckled awkwardly. "I got into Harvard."

Everyone except Darcy erupted into applause and congratulations.

"Are you serious?" Mr. Fitzwilliam looked as though his
smile was about to burst off his face. He turned to his wife.
"Elsie, why didn't you tell me?"

"I wanted it to be a surprise! I wanted to see your face," she
explained. "And it was totally worth it."

"Congratulations, son!" Mr. Fitzwilliam stood and extended
his hand to William, who took it in a formal, practiced manner.
"I can't tell you how proud I am."

"Way to go, baby bro!" said James, patting him on the back.
"Way to do justice to the Fitzwilliam name."

"Justice to the name, indeed," agreed Mr. Fitzwilliam.

"Congratulations," said Kenneth coolly, who himself had
gone to Yale and most likely did not like the idea of relinquish-
ing the title of "Only Fitzwilliam son to have graduated from an
Ivy League university." "I'm sure you'll do great there."

Darcy sat quietly, staring off into space. She didn't understand what the fuss was about. Kenneth had graduated from
Yale and she had graduated from Columbia and James was currently enrolled at Duke University. Both the Fitzwilliam parents
had also gone to Harvard and were the second-richest family in
all of Ohio, and had been for many decades. What did they think,
that William was going to end up at a state school? It seemed to
Darcy that this had been in the cards for some time, and she
couldn't make herself get excited about it. But she noticed her
family was looking to her, as she was the only one present who
hadn't said anything yet.

"Oh." She cleared her throat. "Congratulations, Will. Uh . . .
great job."

"Thanks, Darcy." He nodded to her in a way that made her think maybe he saw it the way she did, and understood. This made her like him better than she had before. That simple nod made him officially her new favorite brother. Actually, she had never had a favorite brother before; she had only disliked them all equally for different reasons. So now William was her *first* favorite brother.

"Okay, Elsie, now tell them the other news."

"There's other news?" William seemed happy to have the attention finally taken off him.

Mrs. Fitzwilliam had an almost mischievous look on her face, like she was enjoying keeping this good news to herself, making everyone squirm.

"Dr. Law came over this morning and says I'm officially out of the woods!" She threw her hands up. "I can go back to living life!"

"Mom, that's incredible!" This time it was Darcy who was first to jump to her feet. She hugged her mom tightly, feeling a weight lift off her shoulders. She hadn't quite realized, until her mom had said these words, how much the fear of losing her had been looming. Unlike the rest of her family, she'd been close with her mother growing up and owed so much of her headstrong determination to that relationship. Had her mom died, Darcy would have felt somewhat like a boat without a rudder.

"Oh, thank God." Mr. Fitzwilliam put his hand over his heart as if it were now he who was having a heart attack. "I don't know what I would have done if I had lost you." He kissed her on the head. "But *honestly*, Elsie, you couldn't have told me this when you first found out?"

"Don't be so dramatic, Don." She laughed at him lovingly. "I only found out an hour ago, and you would have just given away the surprise."

"The surprise that you're not dying?" Kenneth asked, cynically. "Seems to me like that's something you could have told us all immediately."

"Seriously, Mom," said James, "it's not like it's fun to wait in suspense to find out if your mom is on her last legs or not."

"Oh, you know I like to have my fun." She swatted at them like flies. "Don't be such wet blankets!"

"You have a strange idea of fun, my love," said Mr. Fitzwilliam. "Maybe next time you want to have a little fun, we take a trip to Tuscany, instead."

"That's right!" she said excitedly. "That's the whole point, that now that I'm well we actually *can* go to Tuscany. And we should! Should I tell Marianne to book the flights?"

"Whoa, okay, let's not get carried away," James interjected. "Dr. Law just cleared you. I think it's best to take it easy for a little while longer."

"Fine." She rolled her eyes and called into the hallway, "Lorna! Will you bring out a bottle of Dom? We have so much to celebrate."

"Of course, Mrs. Fitzwilliam," Lorna called back. "Coming right up."

"So much for taking it easy," Mr. Fitzwilliam grumbled, defeated.

Lorna came in carrying a bottle of freshly popped Dom Perignon on an elegant silver tray. The cold vapor floated up and around the bottle's neck as she walked. She poured the bubbly liquid into six glasses and the family clinked them together in a fizzy collision.

Darcy's phone buzzed in her pocket. It was a text from Bingley that read, Hey, you free?

She typed back: With family but dying to get out of here. What's up?

The three dots appeared to the right of her screen, and then: Jim ended it. Miserable.

"I'm gonna head out," Darcy told her family, standing from her chair. "Bingley needs me. Congratulations, William! And Mom, I am so relieved, I can't even tell you how relieved I am. See you all tomorrow!"

11

The Charles family lived on the other side of town in a modest-sized ranch-style home with an oversize roof that drooped down over the outer walls, creating a square ring of shade around the perimeter. Bingley was an only child, and his parents were on a ski trip in Stowe, Vermont, and wouldn't be back until late that night.

"Hello?" Darcy called, stepping in through the unlocked front door. "Is anyone home?"

"Yes," Bingley grumbled. "I'm in here."

She followed his voice into the dim living room, lit only by an outside porch lantern. Bingley was sitting on the houndstooth couch with his neck craned back, staring up into the cottage cheese–textured ceiling. On the coffee table in front of him were two miniature bottles of Kahlúa.

"My baby!" she cried, throwing herself down onto the couch next to him. "What happened to you? Tell me everything."

"He said I was right, that things were happening too fast. That he hadn't been thinking clearly and that we should cut it off now, before things get serious. I wanted to get wasted, but all we had here were these two bottles of Kahlúa. They're disgusting." *Ah*, she thought, *so those are* empty *bottles of Kahlúa, then.*

"Well . . . I hate to say it, but don't you think he has a point? I mean, I know I'm the one who introduced you, but I never thought you two would get so crazy and all but move in together within a two-day period, you know? In a way, it's a good idea to break it off now, before you have to go back to L.A. Nobody likes the heartache of a long-distance relationship."

"But I was going to move back to Pemberley, remember? I hadn't even gotten a chance to tell him that yet."

"And that's what you would really want?"

"Oh, I don't know, Darcy." He sighed heavily. "I just didn't want to have to make a decision so soon."

"I get that." She let her head fall back so that it was in line with his. "I wish there was a way we could live on our own timelines without everyone flipping out on us, ya know?"

"Yeah!" He sat up, indignant. "What if I wanted to date long-distantly and see how it went from there? Why does the world gotta be so strict, Darcy?"

"Ha! You had two airplane-size Kahlúas and you're slurring your words like a sailor on leave."

"I'm a pretty little lightweight."

"Well, first things first. We have to get you out of this depressing scene. This whole mess is my fault. I'm the one who told you to cool things down with Jim, and that got him thinking about it in a serious way, and that's on me. But I can fix it. At least I hope I can. Get dressed into something . . . presentable."

"Where we gonna go?"

"Not sure yet. All I know is we won't make any progress lounging around here like two sad potatoes."

"Okay, so I was thinking," Darcy said, pulling Bingley along by his coat sleeve as they trudged down the street in the freezing cold. "The only way for me to fix this is to fix it."

"Uh . . . duh?"

"Don't be a brat. I'm trying to help you."

"Yeah, after you *ruined my life*!" he said with intentional teenage girl affect.

"What a drama queen!"

"Okay, so tell me, you're going to fix it by fixing it how, exactly?"

"You're heartbroken because Jim ended things with you because he was worried your relationship didn't have a future. But the only reason he came up with that is because you told him that you thought things were moving too fast."

"Because *you* told me to!"

"I know, I know, but listen. So I was sitting there in your depressing little living room while you got dressed, trying to think of what we could do to cheer you up. Go out dancing, see a movie, binge eat a box of macaroons, start a Tinder account for you—"

"But I don't want to do any of those things," he whined.

"Exactly. You don't want to do any of those things. All you

want to do is get back together with Jim. So that's what we're going to do: we're going to get you back together with Jim."

"*What?*" He stopped in his tracks.

"Keep walking or we'll freeze to death."

"Why are we walking anyway?"

"I don't know," she admitted. "I didn't think that part through. I was just so excited to get us to the Bennet house that I forgot to think of calling an Uber."

"Darcy," he laughed. "We are not going to the Bennet house."

"Well, why not?"

"What if Jim doesn't want to see me? What if he's not even there? Or worse, what if he's there but with another man?"

"Oh, please. Jim hadn't dated anyone in years until you."

"He just broke up with me; he doesn't want to see me."

"How do *you* know?"

"Generally when someone breaks up with someone else, it means he or she no longer wants to be seeing him or her."

"Bingley! Wake up! He didn't want to break up with you. You forced his hand. And we can unforce it."

"What are you doing?" he asked, noticing that she had taken out her phone and pulled off one glove with her teeth so that she could type.

"I'm calling an Uber. At this rate, we'll never get there." She tapped around and then looked up. "JoJo will be here in two minutes. In a black Prius. Perfect."

"Yeah." Bingley rolled his eyes. "Perfect."

By the time they pulled up at the Bennet house it was almost one o'clock. The house lights were on and, judging by the noise coming from inside, it seemed that most, if not all, of the Bennets were home.

"I don't understand why I can't just call him like a normal millennial would. Or even better, send a text."

"Because this is the romantic way to do it. And this is the only way that it will work. You have to make a gesture big enough to detract from the memory of you saying you want to take space."

"You sound like an expert," he said, stepping out of the Prius.

"Yeah, babe, this isn't the first mess I've had to undo," she said, following him and slamming the black door shut behind them. "Now, which one is his window?"

"Which one is his window?" Bingley stared at her incredulously. "How am I supposed to know?"

"Um, I don't know, weren't you dating the guy?"

"Yeah, for three days."

"Really? Only three days?" She looked back over the short-lived romance. "Maybe I was right. You really were moving too fast."

"*Darcy,*" he scolded, "why are we here?"

"Right. Okay, so the window on the second floor on the far left is Luke's—"

"And wouldn't you know it," he remarked with a smirk.

"Oh, grow up."

"You were saying?"

"The window on the second floor on the far left is Luke's, and the one right next to that is open almost all the way, so . . ." She looked up at the window pensively.

"So . . . so what?" Bingley asked, getting impatient.

"Jim would never let his window stay open in weather like this; he's too conscientious," she explained. "So that means that room must be Kit and Lyle's. Which means the one next to that must be Jim's."

"How do you know? It could be his parents' room! His room could be downstairs! Or he might not even have a room at his parents' house anymore. Maybe they turned it into a gym."

"Well, we won't find out just standing here," she said, bending down and picking up a small stone buried in between frosty blades of grass. She wound her arm back behind her head.

"No! What are you—" Bingley tried to stop her, but it was too late: the stone went flying from her hand, tapping the window she hoped to be Jim Bennet's.

"You're insane," he hissed, then giggled, giddy with adrenaline. They stood in silent anticipation, staring up at the window, which was staying closed.

"Maybe you're right," she said. "Or maybe he's downstairs."

"Or maybe we need to take this as a sign and just go home before one of us gets hypothermia."

Just then, the curtains pulled back and Jim's face was framed in the window. From down below they could see him raise his left eyebrow in confusion. He lifted the window.

"What the hell are you doing down there?" he called down. "Are you drunk?"

"No, actually, weirdly enough, we're sober," Bingley called up. "Although I did have two Kahlúas, but I've probably walked those off by now. So I think it's safe to say that I'm sober, but that's not—"

"Jim," Darcy interrupted, "this is all my fault. I told Bingley he was moving too fast with you. I told him to slow things down. That didn't come from him, that came from me being a jerk. It turns out he doesn't feel that way at all. In fact, I've known him for fourteen years and I've never seen him as happy as he has been in the past few days, since he met you. So now that I've, uh . . . gotten that out of the way, I'm gonna pass this invisible microphone here over to Bingley." She gestured to Bingley hopefully. "Bingley?"

"Yeah, okay." He cleared his throat. "Listen, Jim, when Darcy said I was moving too fast with you I got scared, because I knew she was right."

"I was?" she asked, taken aback.

"Yeah, because, see, we like each other a lot, and that isn't something that happens often. To me, it's happened . . . well . . . never, until now. And I worried that moving fast meant getting to the end sooner, so I wanted to slow it down to make it last longer." He wiped away the sweat that was forming on his brow, even in the cold. "But the truth is, I'm willing to do anything it takes to make this work with you, even though it sounds crazy, and people will tell us we're crazy, but it won't matter. Because it's better to be together in the unknown than apart in the known, where everything is safe. Am I making sense?" Bingley panted. "I feel like I'm having a stroke."

"You're doing great," Darcy said. "That last part was super-poetic, very impressive."

"I'm not talking to you," he panted. "I'm talking to Jim."

"Oh right, of course."

"No," Jim called down. "You're not making sense. But somehow I understand everything you said. I don't want this to end either." He paused, looking around as if for a ladder. "Wait right there; I'll come down."

"Oh my God," Darcy squealed, squeezing Bingley's arm. "It worked! I'm gonna leave you two alone now."

"Thanks, Darcy." He kissed her on the cheek. "Thanks for being crazy and impulsive! This time, it was a great idea!"

"I know!"

She walked away down the street, turning back just once, to see Jim take Bingley's hands in his and swing them side to side. Then she looked up at the window she knew to be Luke's, just as the light went on and the snow began to fall.

12

Darcy walked down to the end of the street to give Jim and Bingley some space. She was proud of what she'd done and was thinking of rewarding herself with a slice of chocolate cake, but she was interrupted when they power walked up behind her.

"What do you lovebirds want?" she joked.

"We're going ice-skating," Bingley said.

"Congratulations," she replied.

"You have to come with us," said Jim.

"Why? You know I'm . . ." She wanted to say "the worst skater of all time" but didn't like the idea of admitting that there were things she wasn't good at it. Owning up to her flaws and weaknesses had never been a strength of Darcy's.

"The worst skater of all time?" Bingley filled in. "Yeah, we know. But it will be fun to watch you fall on your ass a million times."

"Rude!" She laughed.

"Ple-e-ease?" Bingley begged. "I'll buy you hot chocolate with extra marshmallows and I'll win you one of those obnoxious stuffed animals that you like."

"Shh!" She blushed. "You can't tell people these things about me, Bingley. It makes me look all . . . soft."

"Oh, Jim won't tell, right, Jim?"

"Right," Jim agreed. "Plus, I already knew you liked those gigantic bears anyway."

"It's not like you have anything better to do today," Bingley added.

"You don't know that!"

"Oh, so I'm wrong?"

"Ugh." Darcy knew there was no real way out of this. Plus, gliding clumsily around on ice did have some potential for fun, there was no denying it. "Fine. Let's go."

She followed them to Jim's car, thinking that ice-skating might actually be the perfect way to get her mind off the fact that she was powerless against all the goings-on back at the office and that she was supposed to have an answer for Carl soon.

The inside of Chiller Ice Rink was chillingly cold, which was fine by Darcy, as she had come wearing her champagne-colored North Face jacket.

"Why do they have to keep it so cold in here?" asked Bingley, as the three of them stepped out onto the ice. "It's cold enough outside; you would think they'd want to give us a break from that in here."

"Well, they can't have it warm in here," Jim laughed. "The ice would melt."

"A mere technicality," Bingley said with a feigned snobby British accent, holding his chin high.

On wobbly legs, Darcy smiled at her two friends. It was a good idea to come ice-skating. The cold and the clumsiness were worth it, to see the fruits of her matchmaking labors play out successfully. She let them skate ahead while she lingered along the wooden rail that surrounded the circumference of the rink.

Okay, she said to herself, *one step at a time. Easy does it. Just go slowly and you'll be fine.* She inched along, holding on to the rail with one hand. Once she'd gotten used to the feel of being on skates, she attempted to be brave enough to let go. She raised her hand away from the bar and was pleased to see that she could stand on her own. Without the support of the rail, she slid one foot in front of the other, very slowly moving herself forward. *This isn't so hard,* she thought, moving a little bit faster. Gaining confidence, she began to let herself glide along the ice, wondering what she'd thought would be so difficult about this.

"Whoa, look at you!" called Bingley, as he and Jim circled around for the third time.

"Way to go, Darcy!" Jim cheered supportively.

"You guys, I'm really getting the hang of it!" she called out. Just then, in through the sliding doors at the front of the building walked Carl. The suddenness and sheer unpredictability of it caught her so by surprise that she stumbled and fell backward, her butt colliding with hard, cold ice.

"Oh my God, Darcy!" Bingley laughed, skating back around to help her up. "What happened to you?"

Her tailbone was throbbing, but it was nothing compared to the embarrassment of knowing everyone had seen her fall—even Carl and the other guys he was with.

"It's Carl," she said to Bingley, who was holding her tightly by the elbow so that she wouldn't slip again. "Carl Donovan just walked in."

"So?" asked Bingley. "I thought things were whatever between you two?"

"Well, they're not whatever anymore," she said under her breath, as if Carl could hear them. "After my parents' party he gave me an ultimatum. He said I had to decide if we were going to be together, once and for all. If I say no, he's going to move on and not give me any other chances."

"Oh my God," said Bingley. "What are you going to tell him?"

"I don't know yet!" she muttered. "That's why I don't want to see him. Or him to see me."

"It seems like it's too late for that," said Bingley, as Carl came skating over across the ice.

"Fancy running into you here," Carl said, gentlemanly as ever.

"Why did I let you talk me into this?" Darcy muttered to Bingley, under her breath.

"Sorry?" Carl asked.

"Nothing." Darcy smiled. "Bingley and Jim dragged me here today. Wasn't, uh . . . expecting to see you."

"I see you still aren't exactly a pro on the ice." He smiled. "I remember when we came here on a date, junior year. You lost control and slammed right into the—"

"The Plexiglas. Yes, I remember. Great times."

"I'll leave you two to catch up," said Bingley. "Great seeing you, Carl."

"No, Bingley, pl—" She tried to stop him, but it was too late. He was gliding away on the ice, toward Jim. Darcy watched their hands in mittens latch on to each other as they skated away like a pair of turtle doves—whatever the hell those were. Darcy still didn't know.

She looked at Carl and had a flash of the first time she ever saw him, crossing through the science quad at Pemberley High in a black peacoat and beige plaid scarf. She had been drawn to him right away. He had reminded her of a younger, more intelligent looking version of Ben Affleck.

"Looks like you're stuck with me." Carl shrugged. "I can get back to the boys if you prefer." He gestured toward the bleachers, where the guys he had come in with were still lacing up their skates.

"No. It's okay. I know I owe you a conversation."

"Oh, that's okay," he said gently.

"Let's talk now." She thought of the diamond on Charlotte Collins's finger and felt bad for herself that she could ever have thought Luke was an option for her. She had to get realistic.

"Right here?" He seemed surprised, knowing that ice was not among her favorite places to be.

"Yes. Here." She'd avoided Carl long enough, and she longed to get rid of the pent-up guilt she had about the way she had treated him.

"Oh boy." Carl sighed. "This doesn't sound good. You know, I really don't want to rush you. Please take your time and think this through."

"No, Carl, listen . . ." She took his hand in hers. "I *have* been thinking it through. I don't know why I've been fighting this for so long. You were my first . . . well, my first . . . Ugh. You know I hate that word."

"Are you trying to say I was your first *love*?" He stared, bug-eyed and intrigued.

"Yes." She cringed. "As much as I hate to say it, I think it might be true." She knew it wasn't true. But she needed to feel like she was lovable, needed to be with someone who knew what he wanted. And if Carl was nothing else, he was a man who knew what he wanted.

"Wow."

"Yeah, and the only reason I haven't settled down with you is because I don't want to feel dependent on another person. I don't want to be taken care of; I want to take care of myself. But I realize now if I say no to us and lose you, I'll regret it, and I'll regret turning this down in the name of being alone. Because that's what I'll be: alone. So yes, my answer is yes."

"Yes, you want to be with me?" His voice was happy and incredulous like a kid who has woken up on Christmas morning to find that he's received everything he'd ever asked for.

"Yes," she confirmed. "I want to be with you."

With wide, starry eyes he pulled her face in close to his and planted a loving, passionate kiss on her freezing-cold lips.

"You make me so happy," he whispered into her hair.

"You make me happy too." She laughed, realizing that it was almost true. He had never swept her off her feet, but in a very calm, unexciting way, he had made her happy.

"Darcy," he said, pulling his face away from hers, "I have a question."

"Yes?" She searched her brain but couldn't think, for the life of her, what sort of question he'd want to ask her at a time like this. He reached into his jacket pocket and produced a small, blue velvet box.

"Oh my God," she breathed, a tightness wrapping around her throat.

He got down on one knee right there on the cold ice. She was too frozen in shock to try to stop him. She didn't know if she even wanted to stop him. *Maybe this is exactly right,* she thought. *Maybe this is exactly how it's supposed to be.*

"Will you marry me?" He opened the box to reveal a brilliantly shining diamond in the shape of a teardrop fastened onto a polished silver band. It took her breath away. She recognized it: it had belonged to his grandmother, and was just as beautiful as nine years ago, when she'd first seen it. Once upon a time, this ring had been a temptation to fulfill her father's wishes by marrying Carl and therefore marrying into the Donovan family. She had chosen not to give in to the tempting diamond, but the stunning visual of it had never left her mind. It was the kind of diamond you could only say no to once.

"Yes," she said. "I'll marry you."

"Oh my God." He shot back up. "You will?"

"Yes," she laughed. "I want to marry you."

"I can't believe it." His cheeks were turning red, so that

she realized just how pale he'd been only a moment ago. "Okay, well then . . ." He got back down on one knee and slipped the ring onto her finger. She brought her hand up to her face to examine it. It really was lovely, especially with a large expanse of ice as its backdrop. He stood up again so that they were face-to-face.

"It's perfect," she beamed, throwing her arms around his neck and pulling him in for another kiss.

"Whoa, what's going on here?" Bingley asked as he and Jim skated by.

"We're engaged!" Darcy announced, holding up her hand for them to see. Bingley stopped so abruptly that a spray of ice flew up around him.

"Excuse me?" He stared. "Did you just say what I think you just said?"

"I did."

He snatched her hand to get a closer look at the diamond.

"It's so big I could die," he breathed in awe.

"Congratulations, you two," Jim said, pulling each one in for a hug. "This is . . . pretty . . . unexpected, right?"

"Oh, extremely unexpected," said Carl.

"Wildly unexpected," said Darcy.

"I didn't think she'd say yes in a million years."

"And I didn't think he'd propose in a million years!" She laughed. "Well, actually, I knew he would one day, but I didn't think I was even going to see him today, let alone get engaged to him. I mean, just fifteen minutes ago I didn't even know I was going to see him today. I almost didn't even come ice-skating. What if I hadn't? What if I was still alone in my room, trying to figure out what to do today?" She laughed, somewhat manically.

She realized she was on an adrenaline high, so pumped up by the rush of unexpected events that she hadn't had time to process what was going on or to ground herself in reality.

"Your dad is gonna be ha-a-appy," Bingley teased.

"I know," said Darcy. "This is literally all he's wanted for me."

"My parents are going to be thrilled too," said Carl. "They've always been a big fan of Darcy's."

"I know one person who won't be happy," said Jim.

"Who?" asked Darcy.

"My brother."

"*Luke?*" Darcy couldn't believe he'd said it.

"No," said Jim sarcastically. "Kit and Lyle. Yes, Luke."

"Why would Luke care?" Carl asked defensively.

"He wouldn't care," Darcy interjected. "He's engaged to Charlotte Collins. And besides, we don't even like each other."

"I'm sorry," said Jim, realizing he had upset them. "I was joking. I shouldn't have said anything. It's literally nothing. A dumb joke."

"Luke has just always kind of had a crush on Darcy," explained Bingley. "Like, a harmless, schoolboy crush."

"He has *not*," Darcy protested. "He seemed to hate me right up until—"

"Until you made out with him at your parents' Christmas party," Carl realized, pained by the memory that was seared into his mind.

"Right." Darcy blushed, wanting to recoil into her soft turtleneck. "But that was just a drunken thing. It was completely meaningless. Plus, I just saw him with Charlotte. They're super-happy together."

"Sure," said Jim with a hint of pessimism in his voice. "I'm sure they are."

Are they not? Darcy wondered. *And if not, is it possible that—*

No. She interrupted this dangerous train of thought. *You're engaged now. Luke is a thing of the past. A brief, thoughtless fling, and nothing more.*

"Well, that's really none of our business," Carl decided. "It's neither here nor there. Obviously I wish them the best of luck."

"Let's go tell my parents!" Darcy grabbed his hand, trying to change the mood back to a happy one, but that happy feeling was fleeing fast. *Why did I have to come back to Pemberley?* She cursed the circumstances, unable to help but feel grim about her decision. She had been fine in New York. Lonely, sure, but fine. But then she'd come home and had been reminded of Luke and that crazy way he made her feel, that way nobody else had ever made her feel before, and next thing she knew she had totally lost her cool.

"That's a great idea. Are you sure you're ready to do that?"

"Oh, definitely," said Darcy, looking forward to the looks on her parents' faces when she told them. She became painfully aware that she had said yes for all the wrong reasons. She had said yes partially to make her father happy with her again, and partially to run away from whatever the hell had just gone on with Luke. She felt nauseated then, knowing there was no way to undo this.

"Then let's do it," said Carl, turning to Bingley and Jim. "We'll see you guys later!"

"See you later!" They said in unison.

"See you later," said Darcy. Just before she turned away she saw Jim's face and, for the first time, realized how much he looked like Luke. His prominent though elegantly crafted jaw-line and piercingly blue eyes set back in their sockets gave off an air of wisdom. It was a face, she worried, that would be haunting her for years to come.

13

"Oh my God," said Mr. Fitzwilliam. "I think I might faint. I have to sit down."

"Wow, honey," said Mrs. Fitzwilliam, slightly less enthused. "Congratulations!"

Darcy and Carl had just told Mr. and Mrs. Fitzwilliam the news, and both were now having their respective reactions.

"Is this really happening?" asked Mr. Fitzwilliam, sitting down in a brown leather armchair. "Because if it's really happening, well then"—he shook his head—"I'm too pleased for words."

"It's really happening," said Carl. "She said yes!"

Darcy let him drape his arm around her shoulder, which, in front of her parents, she would never let anyone else do. She was warmed by her father's reaction, not realizing until that moment just how much she had always wanted him to approve of her life and her decisions. As a kid she had been close with him. He taught her almost everything she knew, how to swim and hunt and read and tell time. She had missed that feeling of closeness with him but had suppressed these feelings until now, and now that she was standing here, seeing how happy she had made him, the feelings came bubbling up, practically bringing tears to her eyes.

"Well," said Mrs. Fitzwilliam, "we should go out to celebrate, don't you think? How about drinks at Chateau Celeste?"

"Sounds marvelous," said Mr. Fitzwilliam. "Darcy, how 'bout it?"

"I'm game," she said.

"I can't wait to hear everything," said Mr. Fitzwilliam, on the verge of giddiness. "How you proposed, how you planned it, and of course your plans for the wedding."

"I'm thinking a summer wedding, sir," said Carl, which was the first Darcy had heard of this.

"Please," said Mr. Fitzwilliam, "call me Dad."

Call me Dad. The words echoed in Darcy's mind as they sat around the table at Chateau Celeste. Everyone seemed deep in thought about the items on the menu, but Darcy couldn't make herself focus. The first course and the second course and the main course and the side dishes and the desserts and the spirits and the prix fixe all blended together, jumbled in her head, so that she couldn't differentiate between the roasted figs and the wild mushroom risotto and the garlic fingerling potatoes and the traditional free-range tom turkey and the caramelized apple strudel. It could have all been one dish and it wouldn't have made a difference to her. She would barely be able to eat anyway, she knew, with the storm of knots and butterflies brewing in the pit of her stomach.

"The chicken Milanese looks good," said Mr. Fitzwilliam, looking up from the menu. "Should I order one for each of us?"

"Mm, no," said Mrs. Fitzwilliam, "I don't think so. I think I'll have the duck confit salad and then the hanger steak."

"I haven't decided yet," mumbled Darcy, not looking up from the blurring words on the ivory page.

"You can't have the steak, darling," said Mr. Fitzwilliam. "You just had a heart attack . . . you wouldn't think I'd have to remind you so many times."

Mrs. Fitzwilliam stuck her tongue out playfully at her husband.

"The chicken Milanese sounds great," said Carl encouragingly. "I myself would love to try it."

"At least one person is on my side." Mr. Fitzwilliam winked at Darcy. *Gross*, thought Darcy. *If you like him so much, why don't you marry him?*

The waiter came by and Darcy managed to get out that she'd like to order the risotto and a glass of pinot grigio. She didn't really want either, but both had stood out clearly on the menu and so she had committed to them.

"Okay," said Mr. Fitzwilliam, folding his hands on the table. "So you're thinking a summer wedding. I'd suggest June; it's perfect weather here in Pemberley. July and August just get too hot."

"What if we had it in New York?" asked Darcy.

"*New York?*" Her father laughed, confused. "Why would you do that?"

Carl blinked, quietly curious. Aside from ordering food, it was the first thing Darcy had said since they'd arrived.

"Oh," said Darcy, unprepared, "I just sort of always imagined that one day I'd get married at the Plaza. Or at the Boathouse in Central Park."

"Hmm," said Carl. "Interesting."

"Hmm," said her dad. "I hadn't thought of that as an option. I just assumed we would have it in Pemberley so that everyone we know could attend. But I could easily pull some strings to book the Plaza for this summer."

Everyone we know. For this summer. Hearing these words made Darcy begin to feel a little light-headed. The scope and the nearness of this wedding were overwhelming. Especially considering how spontaneous and completely unexpected the engagement had been.

"Well," said Darcy, clearing her throat, "we still have some time to figure that out."

"Not really," said Mr. Fitzwilliam. "Wedding venues book up fast. We should probably lock down a location by this time next week. I'll connect you with Brindy. She plans everybody's weddings these days. Mitch Abernathy said she was an absolute miracle worker during Samantha's wedding. You remember Samantha, from summer camp?"

"Yes," said Darcy, her voice getting stuck in her throat, quiet as a mouse.

The waiter came back with their drinks, placing the glass of white wine in front of Darcy. She picked it up and took a big gulp.

"I was thirsty," she said, when she realized everyone was staring at her.

"Darcy, when are you planning on heading back to New York?" asked Carl.

"Well, I . . . I hadn't really thought about it, actually."

"I was thinking maybe you could get back soon and start looking at venues. Take a look at the Plaza and the Boathouse and see which you like better."

"Mom . . ." Darcy turned toward Mrs. Fitzwilliam. "Are you well enough for me to go home? I don't want to leave until you're one hundred percent definitely going to be fine."

"I'm fine, I'm fine," said Mrs. Fitzwilliam. "It was so amazingly sweet of you to come see me in the first place."

"Are you crazy? You had a heart attack. What kind of daughter would I be if I hadn't come to see you?"

"Well, I'm just very happy that you did."

"Me too," said Carl. "It led you back to me. It's almost like it was meant to be."

Darcy couldn't help but glare at him from across the table. How typical of him, to make her mom's heart attack somehow about him.

"Okay then." Darcy forced a smiled. "I'll go back tomorrow. I've been away from work long enough as it is."

"Perfect," said Mr. Fitzwilliam. "I'll have my assistant put you in touch with Brindy, and also Monty Bismarck—he's my connection at the Plaza."

"Great." Darcy stared into her now more than half-empty wineglass. She took out her phone and started looking up the earliest flights out of Pemberley.

14

"I'm surprised your parents were okay with me spending the night," said Carl, unbuttoning the collar of his shirt. They were alone in Darcy's childhood bedroom, sitting on the foot of the bed. She had booked a flight for ten the next morning and had invited Carl to be with her on her last night in Pemberley. It seemed like the polite thing to do, considering he was her fiancé now.

"Please," said Darcy. "They've been waiting for this for eight years. At least my dad has."

"Still, I wouldn't think your dad would want me sleeping in our bed *out of wedlock*."

"He can be surprisingly liberal from time to time," she said. "And besides, he's basically in love with you. In a noncreepy way, I mean."

"Well, that's all fine and good," said Carl, inching closer to her on the bed. "But all I really care about is if you're in love with me."

Dammit, thought Darcy. *He's drawn attention to the elephant in the room.*

She responded by kissing him on the mouth and hastily unbuttoning the rest of the buttons on his starched Ralph Lauren dress shirt. It was better than having to talk about whether she was in love with him, a conversation that would no doubt be awkward, considering not even she knew the answer. He kissed her back, running his hands through her hair.

"Ouch," Darcy said, reacting to a sharp pain on her scalp.

"What's wrong?" he asked.

"Nothing . . . just, my hair got stuck on your finger and you pulled and it was just, like, bad for a second, but it's fine now."

"Oh, okay," he said, pausing to study her face, as if waiting for a cue telling him what to do next.

"You can keep kissing me," she said.

"Okay," he sighed, relieved, and went back to kissing her, this time with his hands on her shoulders for safe measure.

From their very first kiss until now, his kissing technique had evolved in no way whatsoever. It had always been good, sure, but not incredible. It was nice, practiced, wholesome, almost regulated. He had reliable rhythm and predictable moves. Rhythm and moves that she enjoyed but that lacked the excitement she longed for. The excitement she got when she was kissing Luke.

No, she interrupted herself, *don't even think about going there.*

To keep herself from thinking about Luke, she continued pulling at Carl's clothes until they were all the way off. Impatiently, she let him undress her. He tried to pull her shirt up over her head, but it snagged on one of her earrings.

"Wait, wait," he said. "I'll get it." He furrowed his brow, examining the place where the earring and shirt fabric intertwined, and got to work untangling them.

"Forget it," she said. "I'll just take my earring out." She slid the gold post out of the hole in her ear and threw the earring-shirt tangle onto the bed. He reached around her ribs to unhook her bra but Darcy didn't want to wait, so she pushed his hands away and did it herself. It's not that she was dying to get into bed with Carl but that every second it was getting harder and harder to put Luke out of her mind, and she felt compelled to rush the action forward, as if the speed might leave Luke and his memory in the dust. But she soon found that she was wrong. Nothing she did could successfully block out the thought of Luke, and she fell asleep next to her fiancé, wondering how on earth she had gotten herself into this mess.

When the sun rose, Darcy got dressed quietly, careful not to wake Carl, who was sleeping deeply, with a soft smile on his lips. *Lucky, naive jerk,* she thought, finding that she envied him. He knew what he wanted *and* he had gotten it. Meanwhile, Darcy had no idea what she really wanted or what she should do about it, and she worried that she never would. *And if I never figure out what I want, I'll never be able to even begin going about getting it,* she thought, *and then will I just be trapped in a limbo of dissatisfaction for the rest of my life?*

For a second, the fear paralyzed her, but then Carl's arm twitched and he rolled over, and the fear that he'd wake up before she could get out eclipsed the first fear. She put on her peacoat and took a pen and paper from her vanity station.

Carl,
By the time you read this I'll be on the plane to New York. I look forward to seeing you there soon. Will keep you posted about the Plaza.
    XO, Darcy

She lugged her suitcase down the elegantly curved staircase and found Edward waiting for her in the foyer. He looked bright and cheery as always.

"To the airport, then?" He smiled.

"Yes, please." Darcy nodded, feeling the rims of her eyes stinging with exhaustion.

"Are you all right?" Edward asked, taking her suitcase. "You seem . . ."

"I had a hard time sleeping," she said, following him out the front door and onto the cobblestone driveway. "It's been a long week."

"Looking forward to being back in the Big Apple?"

"More than you know." She smiled. "Hey, you should come visit me there sometime."

"Me?" He laughed, opening the black car's back door for her. "What would *I* do in New York City?"

"Lots of stuff," she said. "You'd love it."

"Maybe one day," he said, humoring her, then shut the door and got into his seat.

"Partition open or closed?" he asked.

"Open," she said. "I barely got to see you this whole trip."

"Open it is, then," he said, seemingly pleased.

"You know," she began, curious to see how he'd react, "I might be getting married in New York."

At first he said nothing, but from the look in his eyes, which she could see in the rearview mirror, he might as well have slammed on the brakes. Edward was not a brake-slamming type of man, and so instead he said calmly, "Who's the lucky man?"

"Carl Donovan," she said. "You've met him."

"A very nice young man." Edward nodded.

"Do you think I should do it?"

"Do what?"

"Marry him."

"You're asking me if you should marry Carl Donovan?"

"Yes."

"You've already said yes, haven't you?"

"Yes, but . . . Edward, I don't know."

"What don't you know?" he asked. "Why wouldn't you marry him?"

"Because I'm not . . ." She paused. "I'm not in love with him." She heard the words come out of her mouth and was shocked by them. She'd never said this out loud, and certainly wasn't expecting to say it for the first time to Edward.

"Oh dear." Edward was clearly not expecting this either.

"What? If I don't love him, I shouldn't marry him?"

"I can see how you'd think I might say that." He smiled sadly. "But the truth is there are reasons to marry someone even if you're not in love with them. There are financial reasons, though I hardly think that's the case here; there are familial obligations; there are biological purposes—let's say you're ready to start a family, for example. Some people are romantic types, you know?

They want to hold out for that one special person that they know is out there, but others are more practical. Neither is right or wrong; it's just a matter of who you are and what you want for yourself. Do you want to spend the rest of your life with someone who you get along with perfectly well but you're not in love with, or would you rather be alone until the love of your life shows up? There's pros and cons to both, my dear."

She felt her heartbeat rise with an odd combination of panic and excitement.

"What if the love of your life is already in your life?" she blurted.

"Uh, well . . ." Edward was no doubt confused. "Then you should be with that person. Life is short. Why would you not be with someone you're in love with?"

"Edward, we have to make a quick stop."

"Oh?"

"It's on the way. It won't take long, I promise."

Edward chuckled.

"It can take as long as you want," he reminded her. "I just don't want you to miss your flight."

"If I do," she said, "it will be worth it.

As soon as they pulled up at the Bennet house, Darcy flung her door open.

"I'll be back soon," she told Edward, though in truth she had no plan and no idea how this was all about to play out. The sky was gray and there was a light drizzle that dampened her hair as she made her way to the front door.

What are you doing? a sharp voice inside her head hissed at her, as she raised her finger to the doorbell. *I'm doing what I have to do,* she hissed back at it, and rang the doorbell. Just as she did so, the rain picked up speed and started falling heavily.

The door opened and there was Jim, wearing a festively green cardigan.

"Darcy? What are you doing here? It's pouring!"

"It wasn't a second ago," she said, her teeth starting to chatter.

"Come in, come in," he said, pulling her inside.

The Bennet house smelled of gingerbread and burning wood. It was a comforting smell that made her feel at home, although her family home smelled nothing like it. The Fitzwilliam home smelled chronically clean, like Clorox and artificial pine needles.

"Is Luke here?" Darcy asked. She realized suddenly that Charlotte might be here with him and cursed herself for her own impulsivity. She hadn't planned this at all, and she was scared, but she knew what Edward had said would haunt her if she didn't do *something.*

"Yeah," said Jim. "He's just in his room, I'll go get him."

"Thank you," Darcy panted, both relieved and nervous.

"Great, wait right here," said Jim, hurrying up the stairs.

Minutes later, Luke came down the stairs with a furrowed, confused brow. He raised an eyebrow at Darcy.

"Darcy . . . ?" He looked her up and down, trying to understand what was going on. "Is everything all right? You look like a wet sewer rat who's just seen a ghost."

"Thank you? Everything's fine," she assured him hurriedly, worried that Jim might come back downstairs at any moment. "Look, it's just . . . Hi." She smiled awkwardly.

"Hi," he said back. "You're freaking me out."

"Okay, so here's the thing. I'm just going to say it." She took a deep breath. "On paper, you are totally wrong for me—you have no ambition and we don't even have anything in common—and yet . . . and yet I find I love you."

Her heart beat frantically. She could feel it banging up against the inside of her neck like a frantic and frenzied bird against a glass window. Luke's eyes widened and he took a small step back.

"I'm engaged," he said.

"I know, I know, and I am too." She lifted up her hand to show him the ring. "Carl proposed, and I said yes. But the thing is, Luke—"

"Oh my God," he said, a look of disgust spreading across his face. "You're even worse than I thought."

"What?" She felt the blood drain from her face. The warmth she normally saw deep in his eyes was gone and he was completely shut off from her, like a steel door.

"You're so incredibly self-centered and selfish. You don't know what love is, Darcy. If you knew what love was, you wouldn't barge in here and try to tear up my relationship. You're not thinking of me, or of Charlotte, and definitely not of Carl. All you're thinking about is yourself."

"But I—" Darcy stammered and froze. She couldn't believe what she was hearing. She thought, at worst, he would kindly brush off her declaration of love. She hadn't imagined anything like this. This was brutal.

"You're so obsessed with yourself," he went on. "You think you can do and say whatever you want because you're so much better than everyone. You look down on everyone and everything. Your pride is off the charts, and it's just too much for me to take. You're a snobby New Yorker, and you should go back to the city and leave me alone."

"Oh." Darcy put her hand to her cheek as if she had been slapped in the face. "Well then, that's exactly what I'll do."

She took a deep breath and put every ounce of energy she had into giving Luke a polite, composed smile. Then she turned away, avoiding eye contact with Jim, who had reappeared at the bottom of the staircase. She walked slowly, in a daze, back to the town car. Once inside, with the door closed behind her, she rested her head against the window and tried not to cry.

15

Back in her New York loft-style apartment, Darcy hid in bed, deep under luxurious, Egyptian-cotton linens and a three-thousand-dollar European goose down comforter. The phone by her side kept lighting up with texts from Bingley and Carl and her brothers, and even one from Jim, but she ignored them all. Especially the ones from Carl. Of course, Carl didn't know that she had gone to Luke's house to make a total fool of herself, but she was so ashamed of herself that she worried that talking to him now would push her over the edge into officially hating herself.

This feeling was a completely new one for Darcy. It's not that Darcy had always been an upbeat kind of girl, but she had always, always thought highly of herself. Even in her darkest hours she never blamed herself or worried that she was the problem. Sure, people at work or people she didn't know at all had called her a snob and other horrible things, but nobody whose opinion she cared about, and definitely nobody she loved. Until now, names she'd been called had always been water off a duck's back, but Luke's words were sticking. He was right, she was self-centered and egotistical, and it was true, aside from a select few, she really did only care about herself.

As for thinking she was better than everybody else, was that really so wrong? She played this one over and over again in her mind. Didn't everybody think they were better than everybody else? If life is a competition, then you are your own team, and if you want to win—i.e., survive—you have to believe that your team—i.e., you—is the best. Right?

She burrowed deeper beneath the blankets, wondering what she was missing. Was she actually supposed to believe that everybody was created equally? To Darcy, there was evidence running rampant that this was simply not the case.

It doesn't matter, she told herself. *It doesn't matter what Luke thinks of you. You're getting married to Carl, and he thinks you're perfect just the way you are.* She picked up the phone she'd been shamefully avoiding and read the text from Carl.

When is your appointment to look at the Plaza? it read.

Today at 5, she replied.

Amazing, he wrote. I'm flying in today at noon, I'll get to see it with you!

Hooray! she typed, then searched for the right emoji. Her thumb hovered over the skull for a second, but she ended up going with an unrealistic amount of heart-eyed faces, then let her phone drop listlessly onto the mattress.

The good thing about her anxiety about marrying Carl was that it distracted her from the epic devastation of Luke not only rejecting her but also tearing apart her character and entire sense of self-worth. There was one other thing that could distract her: work. She picked her phone back up and called Millie.

"Darcy!" she answered cheerily. "We haven't heard from you in so long!"

"I know," said Darcy. "Sorry about that." There was a moment of silence from Millie's end. Darcy wondered if it was caused by the shock of hearing her say sorry for the first time.

"That's okay. You're the boss!" Millie assured her. "You can do whatever you want."

"Thanks, Millie," said Darcy. She'd never been able to tell if Millie was a genuinely sweet girl or if she was just an expert at acting like one. "Listen, I'm back in New York and will come by today, in an hour."

"Really? You know, it's Christmas Eve. Barely anyone is here. Of course, feel free to come in—you're the boss, like I said—but there's really not much going on here."

"That's okay." Darcy began to fantasize about having the office all to herself. "I'll just catch up on some phone calls."

"Whatever you say!"

"See you soon, Millie."

Darcy hung up the phone and had an idea. Luke said she was self-obsessed? Well, would a self-obsessed person think to buy her assistant a very expensive Christmas present?

"I think *not*," she said out loud, to nobody.

On her way into the office, Darcy stopped at Tiffany's. She hurried awkwardly past the wedding ring collection and on to the necklaces, where she browsed quickly, looking for the most beautiful, elegant one. She settled on the diamond solitaire pendant, fourteen karat white gold.

"That one, please!" She pointed to it so the attendant wearing all beige—lipstick included—could see it. Darcy delighted in watching the attendant pluck the necklace from the white velvet display shelf and slip it into the Tiffany-blue suede pouch, which was then slipped into a Tiffany-blue box and tied with a white silk bow. As adults, nobody talked much about their favorite color, and Darcy couldn't think of the last time anybody had asked about hers, but if they did, she'd no doubt tell them Tiffany blue.

"Wow," Darcy said, walking in through the heavy glass door and into her corner office at Montrose Montrose and Fitzwilliam. "You weren't kidding. It really is dead around here." Millie was sitting on Darcy's couch with her laptop open, typing furiously. When she saw Darcy come in, she stopped midtype to look up. Millie was a nice-looking girl, charmingly naive, with thin-rimmed glasses, dark brown hair that she kept in a bun, and a penchant for cardigans, which she seemed to own in every shade of every color.

"Darcy!" She shot up from her seat. "Welcome back."

"Thanks, Millie. It's good to be back."

"Here are your messages," Millie said, scurrying to produce a stack of papers from beneath a different stack of papers. "And I can brief you on the clients whenever you're ready."

"Don't worry about that." Darcy smiled.

"What?" Millie tilted her head to the side, taken aback. "What do you mean?"

"We can do all that later. It's Christmas Eve. We don't need to do any work right now."

"But then . . . why did you come in?"

"I have a present for you."

"For me?" Millie stared. She looked as if Darcy had just told her she'd been selected at random to have dinner with the president.

"Yes, for you. Is that really so crazy?"

"No, no . . . I mean . . . uh . . . It's just you've never gotten me a present before."

"I know," said Darcy. "You've been working for me for three years and I've never even gotten you a birthday present. It's completely unforgivable."

"Well, now, no, that's not true," Millie offered generously. "You wrote me a card two years ago on my birthday."

"That's pathetic." Darcy rolled her eyes at herself. "I'm the absolute worst. I've been so self-centered, and I gotta change that. Something has to change. So here. I hope this is a good step in the right direction."

Darcy slipped the blue box out of her Chanel bag and held her arm out to Millie.

"Oh my God, Darcy," Millie laughed. "You're kidding me, right? You got me something from Tiffany's?"

"Open it! Well, wait, it has a card. Read that first."

Millie opened the white card attached to the box and read it out loud.

"'Happy Holidays to the perfect assistant. Sincerely, the Darcy-cuda.'" Millie turned bright red.

"I . . ." she stammered, embarrassed. "I didn't think you, uh . . . I didn't think you knew about that nickname. And we mean it as a compliment."

"We?" Darcy raised an eyebrow, amused. "I thought it was just you."

This made Millie redden even more.

"Oh, no, well, I mean, it's not like—"

"Millie, relax." Darcy rested her hand on Millie's shoulder. "I'm not mad and I'm not going to make you tell me who else calls me that. I take it as a compliment. In fact, you can keep calling me that."

"Really?"

"Yeah, it's sweet. I guess I like that you know me well enough to come up with a nickname. And one that actually fits."

"Oh." Millie shrugged, relaxing slightly. "Okay."

The two eyed each other uneasily, each unsure how to read the other, then broke out laughing.

"And I'll come up with one for you, but I'll need some time to think. So now open your present!"

Millie pulled on the white ribbon and it slid effortlessly off the box. She took the top off and looked inside. Her eyes widened to the size of Christmas ornaments.

"You're crazy," she balked. "You didn't."

"I did! Do you like it?"

"Do I like it? It's the most beautiful thing I've ever seen."

"Here," said Darcy. "I'll help you put it on." She plucked the necklace out of the cotton padding inside the box and unclasped it, then hung it around Millie's neck so that it fell perfectly over her collarbones. Then she directed Millie by the shoulders to the nearest mirror, so she could see the diamond glittering from the center of her chest.

"It looks incredible on you!"

"It would look incredible on anyone. It's a frickin' diamond."

"Well, it's perfect for you, and it's yours, so enjoy!"

"I got you something too," Millie confessed. "Of course, it isn't a diamond, and probably costs one-twentieth of what you got me." She went to the bookshelf and brought back a lumpy object wrapped in gold wrapping paper.

"Oh, please," joked Darcy. "I have enough diamonds. And it's the thought that counts anyway, right?"

"Sure," Millie agreed bashfully. "Here. I hope you like it."

"I know I will," Darcy said, tearing into the paper with her acrylic nails. Inside was a scarf, beautifully and elaborately hand-knitted in gradational shades of purple.

"Millie! I love it," Darcy said, genuinely, and wrapped it around her neck. "Where's it from?"

"I made it."

"Stop!" Darcy gasped, eyeing her reflection in the mirror. "You are so amazingly talented. How long have you been knitting?"

"Oh . . ." Millie thought. "About fifteen years. Actually I . . . I've knitted something for you every Christmas that I've worked here."

"You have?" Darcy searched her crowded memory but came up with nothing. "Why haven't I received them?" For a moment she thought to call her assistant and yell at her for not making sure she got the presents each year, but then remembered that Millie *was* her assistant, and this definitely wasn't *her* fault.

"I think they normally just get lost in the pile of stuff clients send you. It's not a big deal, though. They're just scarves."

"Well, it's a big deal to me," said Darcy. "It's an honor to be wearing something made by somebody so important to me."

Three hours later, Darcy and Carl walked up Fifth Avenue toward the Plaza Hotel. Snow was falling lightly, and Carl kept rubbing her arms to keep her warm. *It's nice that he cares about my comfort*, she thought. *That's a good quality in a husband, no doubt. Although I don't actually want him to be rubbing my arms, and he can't intuit that, and an inability to read me is not a good quality in a husband.*

They walked up the front steps and were greeted by a woman in a pink wool pantsuit and oversize pearl earrings.

"You must be Carl Donovan and the future Mrs. Carl Donovan," she said, way too sweetly for Darcy's taste. "I'm Brindy."

Of course you are, thought Darcy.

"Hi, Brindy!" Carl extended his hand politely. "I'm Carl and this is my fiancée, Darcy Fitzwilliam."

Good, thought Darcy, *he knows I hated that she called me "the future Mrs. Carl Donovan" and he is working to correct her. He remembers in senior year when I said if I ever got married I would keep my own last name. Good memory, respects my wishes—those are some good points in his favor.*

"Hi." Darcy gave her a weak wave. "Nice to meet you."

"The pleasure is all mine, I'm sure." Brindy clutched a clipboard close to her plump chest. "If you'll just follow me, I'll show you around so you can see what a gem this place is. As you know, your father is an old friend of Monty's, so you could easily book this place for a steal."

"Money isn't an object," Darcy said, tucking a strand of hair behind her ear, then thinking, *It's things like that that make people think I'm a snob, isn't it?*

"Even so . . ." Brindy gave her a strained smile. "It's always nice to have connections." She led them through a foyer and into the main lobby, which was currently overflowing with tastefully elegant Christmas decorations: white-branched trees wrapped in white lights, a robust tree threatening to go through the ceiling, a Santa's Village display made of gingerbread and fondant icing, replete with a glazed sugar ice rink on which plastic figurines were skating.

"The Plaza can host two hundred wedding guests, not to mention the convenience of having rooms upstairs for anyone who wants to spend the night," Brindy recited. "Many couples who have their weddings here also like to open up the Oak Room for drinks during the reception, so the guests can drift in and out casually, as they please."

"Great," said Carl. "So what about the—"

"We'll take it," Darcy interrupted.

"We will?" Carl was taken aback. "Don't you want to check out the Boathouse at Central Park? Or at least, don't you have any questions for Brindy?"

"Nah." Darcy shrugged. "What's there to ask? It's gorgeous and I've wanted to get married here for as long as I can remember. I don't see why we need to drag out the process of choosing a place." This was a lie. Darcy had never imagined herself getting married, let alone imagined the venue, but she would have said anything to minimize the amount of energy spent on the wedding-to-be. The more attention she gave it, the more real it would become.

"Wow," said Brindy, impressed. "Most women tend to overthink these things when preparing for their wedding."

"Yeah, well," said Darcy, "I'm not most women. And I like making snap decisions. It's helped me get ahead in life, and I don't plan on stopping any time soon. How much is the deposit?"

"Oh, you don't have to worry about that, Darcy," said Carl. "Your father is taking care of that."

"Why?" asked Darcy. "I'm independently wealthy and I have my checkbook right here."

"I'll just text Monty," Brindy said, clearly unnerved by Darcy's determined, agitated energy. Actually, even Darcy herself was disturbed by it. "He can come down from his office and talk numbers."

"Yes," said Darcy, feeling her cheeks grow hot with adrenaline. "You do that."

"So," said Carl. They were sitting at the Oak Room bar, drinking martinis. Darcy rushed through the first one so that she could move on to the second.

"So?" asked Darcy.

"You made that decision pretty fast."

"What decision?"

"On the Plaza."

"No." Darcy shook her head and took a sip. "It was a decision made over the course of twenty years. I was nine when I first thought one day I'd have my wedding at the Plaza."

"Well, okay then."

"Okay then."

"It just seems like . . ." He trailed off, looking around the bar as if worried that he was being watched. Darcy braced herself for what she knew he was about to say next. "It just seems like you're rushing things a little bit. Are you sure you . . . Are you sure you want to do this?"

"Do what?" She didn't know what else to do, other than play dumb.

"Marry me."

"What?" She laughed. "Of course I want to marry you. Otherwise, why would I have said yes?"

"I don't know," he began. "Maybe because—"

Darcy's phone began to vibrate. It was a call from her brother. *Ah,* she thought, relieved, *saved by the bell.*

"James, hi," she answered the phone, then mouthed to Carl, *Be right back,* and stepped outside into the freezing-cold New York afternoon.

"Hey, Darcy," James said. "How's New York? Happy to finally be back?"

"Sure," said Darcy. "It's . . . you know, New York. Pretty time of year and all that. What's up?"

"Just wondering if you'd heard about the Bennets." His voice sounded calm enough, so she held back her immediate reaction of fear and concern.

"Which Bennets?"

"Kit and Lyle."

"No, I haven't heard. What happened to them? Is everything okay?"

"It's not a huge deal, but they were caught vandalizing the school, those little punks, and now they're going to be expelled. Mr. and Mrs. Bennet are beside themselves, obviously."

"How's Luke?"

"Luke? He's fine."

"Okay . . . why are you telling me this?"

"No reason really," he said. "Before you left, you told me to keep you in the loop. This is me keeping you in the loop."

Darcy laughed, amused by the idea that anyone in her family was ever actually listening to her, let alone responding to her words.

"Well, thank you, James, I appreciate it. How are you doing?"

"Me? Same old. We miss you, though."

"I miss you too," said Darcy, and meant it. "Talk soon?"

"Yeah, talk soon."

Darcy hung up the phone and took a deep breath, feeling the icy air fill up her lungs, then slowly made her way back inside and took her seat at the bar next to Carl.

"That was my brother," she said. "James."

"What did he say?"

"He called to tell me that Kit and Lyle Bennet got expelled for vandalizing the school."

"That's strange."

"Not really," said Darcy. "They've pretty much always been delinquents."

"No, I mean weird that he called to tell you that."

"I guess. I think he just misses me."

"Oh," said Carl. "That's sweet. I guess."

"You guess?"

"It's odd to me that he'd keep you updated on the Bennet family. Why would he think you'd care about what's going on with them?"

"He doesn't think I'd care about what's going on with them," Darcy said, irritated. "I told him to keep me updated on things in Pemberley. He was just doing what I asked him to."

"And why do you want to be updated on what's going on in Pemberley? You haven't thought twice about Pemberley in a decade . . . I guess I just don't understand why now."

"How about because my mom is sick? Because I reconnected with my family for the first time since college? Did you ever think maybe I actually liked my time in Pemberley? Would that really be so hard to believe? Not to mention, Bingley will be living there now with Jim."

"Ah yes, Jim," said Carl, crumpling up a cocktail napkin in his hand.

"Yes?" asked Darcy. "What about Jim?"

"Another Bennet," replied Carl, smugly.

"What's your sudden problem with the Bennets?"

"First of all, it isn't with the Bennets, it's with Luke Bennet. And second of all, it isn't sudden. I haven't liked him since early high school, when I could tell he had a thing for you and—"

"Luke did not have a thing for me in high school," Darcy protested. "He wasn't even nice to me in high school."

"Yes," said Carl. "Exactly. He liked you but he didn't know what to do about it, so he treated you terribly, and I hated him for that."

"Oh." This was new information to Darcy. She reflected on her life, wondering what she might have done had she known Luke liked her in high school.

"But apparently you like being treated terribly, because now he's become your little make-out buddy."

"We kissed twice," said Darcy, outraged. "And I was drunk both times. You do know he's engaged, don't you?"

"I do know that, and if I didn't know any better, I'd say the only reason you agreed to marry me was because he suddenly wasn't an option."

"How could that possibly be true? I've been dating you forever and just kissed him for the first time a week ago! I never had feelings for him before that."

Darcy heard the words come out of her mouth and tried to screech them to a halt, but it was too late. There they were, out on the table.

"I mean I—" She tried to backpedal, but Carl interrupted her.

"So you do have feelings for him," he said, nodding, more sad than mad.

"I . . . I think I might. Or at least I did. But he hates me now, so it doesn't even matter, it's a moot point. Look, Carl, what you and I have is so—"

"Why does he hate you now?" Carl interrupted again.

"Oh . . ." Darcy shrugged and tried not to cry. "He says I'm a snob and that I think I'm better than everyone else."

"Well," said Carl, sitting back in his chair, "he's not wrong, is he?"

16

Darcy woke in the middle of the night with a pounding heart and sweat trickling down her forehead. Carl was sleeping soundly next to her in her California king–size bed. Why hadn't he ended it with her right then and there, once he found out about her complicated feelings for Luke? She didn't understand. But sitting up in the dark with her heart flopping like a fish out of water, she knew she was going to have to take action. If she wanted to ever feel at peace again, she was going to have to do the right thing.

Quietly, she slipped out of bed and into her study, where she found a sheet of her own stationery and a black fountain pen. She paused, realizing this was the second time in a week that she was leaving Carl with nothing but a note, and she felt guilty. She wondered if she should stay put and stick to the plan of marrying him, but that thought made her feel even guiltier. She couldn't live that deep in dishonesty and feel okay about it.

> Dear Carl,
>
> I am so sorry to do this to you, but as cruel as it seems, it is kinder than if I had gone through with the marriage. I know you think we are supposed to be together, and I know our families certainly think so too, but I know in my heart that this isn't right, and I have to honor that. You deserve better than me, someone who is certain about you. You're a one-of-a-kind gentleman and you deserve the best. I sincerely hope that we can stay friends.
>
> Love, Darcy.

She slipped the note into an envelope and wrote "I'm sorry" in big letters on the front, so that he'd understand immediately. *Oh,* she thought then, *what if when he reads this he's so furious that he trashes my apartment? What if he steals from me? What if he breaks all my things? Maybe I should reconsider. Wait until he wakes up, tell him in a public place.* She mulled this over in her mind as she started throwing some clothes into her suitcase. *Nah,* she decided, *if he trashes my place, I'll get a new place and new stuff to go in it. All I know is I gotta get out of here immediately, before I change my mind.*

She packed everything she needed, used her phone to hastily book a flight, left the envelope on the nightstand, then stealthily snuck out of the apartment as she'd done before and hoped never to do again. She'd take a red-eye and be in Pemberley by daybreak.

———————

She didn't want to make a big fuss about returning to Pemberley— she didn't need people asking questions—so she didn't bother to tell Edward she was coming to town. She hopped in the first cab she could get and gave the driver directions to Bingley's parents' house.

Bingley, she texted, I'm back in town, can I stay at your folks' for the night, I'll explain later.

Explain now, he wrote back immediately. I'm intrigued!

Darcy rolled her eyes and started to type.

Darcy: I called things off with Carl. I'm back in town to take some space and clear my head. I don't want to stay at my parents' because I'm not ready to tell them what happened.

Bingley: Oh, girl. Are you gonna be okay? My parents are gone, take as much time as you need.

Darcy: I'll be fine. A little shaken up right now. Are you with Jim?

Bingley: Not at the moment, but we're very much together. Why?

Darcy: How is he holding up after what happened to Kit and Lyle?

Bingley: Worried. He doesn't want them to have to go to juvenile hall. This was their last strike.

Darcy: Ah. That's stressful.

Bingley: You're just dying to ask me how Luke is doing, I can tell.

Darcy: Oh, shut up.

Bingley: He's pretty distressed about his brothers. He practically raised them, you know, so he feels partly responsible for what's happened.

Darcy: I didn't ask!

Darcy put her phone facedown and a plan began to formulate in her mind. She found herself experiencing a series of feelings she had never felt before. First there was compassion, compassion for people who didn't affect her life in any way. In the past she never would have cared what happened to Kit and Lyle, as it had no impact on her whatsoever. But now she found that she cared; the thought of them going to juvenile hall made her sad. It made her sad for Luke and Jim, mostly, whom she now cared for, whether they cared for her or not.

Then there was a feeling of wanting to take action for the benefit of other people, even though it would do nothing for her personally, other than the knowledge that she had helped. In the past, "feeling good about helping" was not an emotion she experienced. Even the few times she'd done volunteer work, she'd taken no real satisfaction from helping others. Either she worked toward bettering her own life and position or she didn't work at all. And now she knew helping Kit and Lyle would do nothing for her—there was no financial reward, and it certainly wouldn't change the way Luke felt about her—but she found that she wanted to do it anyway. She wanted to help Kit and Lyle get out of juvenile hall just for the sake of making people's lives better.

As the taxi swerved along the country road, Darcy was struck by how differently she felt now from when she had first arrived back in Pemberley a week ago. Then, it had been eight years since she'd been there, and it had felt like entering a foreign, disorienting land. Now, looking out the foggy taxi window at the trees and winding road, it felt like home.

Darcy walked up the front steps of Pemberley High, a place she hadn't been since graduation day, eleven years ago. She knew it was unlikely that anyone would be here on Christmas, but she'd only scold herself later if she didn't at least try. The steps were wet and slippery with half-melted snow, so she had to be careful climbing in her velvet Manolo Blahnik heels. She walked in through the front entrance and down the main hall, past the rows and rows of lockers, which had gone from elephant gray to upbeat orange since the last time she had seen them. She didn't know who exactly she was looking for, but she knew she had to get ahold of someone with authority.

The principal, she thought. *Of course. Mr. Hastings will be happy to help me. I was his star student for four whole years.* She let her memory zigzag her confidently through the hallways and to Mr. Hastings's frosted glass window. *Please be here, please be here!* she thought, crossing her fingers as she walked.

"Oh," Darcy said, as she came face-to-face with the window that no longer read "Mr. Hastings" but instead read "Mrs. Walsh." She noticed a flurry of anxiety rise up from her stomach, which was her third or fourth new feeling of the day. At first she didn't like it, mistaking it for cowardice, something she'd never demonstrate. Then she noticed how it made her feel alive, and she was more than up to the challenge.

What are you worried about? she asked herself, standing outside the door. *You talk to new people all the time. You're fantastic at it. You're confident and brilliant and you know how to get what you want.*

She turned the brass knob and pushed the door open. There she was faced with a grumpy-looking woman who reminded her somewhat of a frog, sitting at a wood-paneled kiosk.

"Um, hi!" Darcy tried, with a pleasant smile. "I'm here to speak with Mrs. Walsh."

"Is she expecting you?" the woman croaked, looking up over the top of her thick-rimmed glasses. Darcy saw that the woman's name tag read "Linda."

"No, she's not, actually. But hi, Linda, I'm Darcy Fitzwilliam. I'm an alumna of Pemberley High and I have a matter of importance that I'd like to discuss with Mrs. Walsh."

"I'll see if she's available," Linda said, shuffling some papers and reaching for the phone. "Hi, Mrs. Walsh," she spoke into the receiver. "I have a Miss Fitzwilliam here to see you. She says it's a *matter of importance*." She said these last words like they were the most ridiculous words she'd ever heard. "Okay, I'll send her back." She hung up the phone with a heavy click.

"You can go on back. It's the last door to your left."

"Thank you." Darcy bowed her head in appreciation and followed Linda's direction to the last door on the left, which was cracked open slightly. Darcy knocked.

"Come in!" said a voice, much friendlier than Linda's. Darcy pushed the door open and saw Mrs. Walsh sitting at her desk, a long-legged woman with excellent posture who seemed no older than forty-five.

"Hi," said Darcy, extending her hand. "I'm Darcy Fitzwilliam." Mrs. Walsh stood briefly to shake her hand, then sat back down.

"I'm Mrs. Walsh," she said. "But you can call me Dawn. Please, have a seat." She gestured to the couch on the opposite end of the room. Darcy took a seat.

"Nice to meet you, Dawn."

"So what can I help you with today?"

"It's about the Bennet boys, Kit and Lyle."

"Oh boy." Dawn whistled. "Those poor boys."

"Yes!" said Darcy. "Exactly. They're so . . . misguided. And—"

"I'm sorry, are you a relative of theirs?"

"An old family friend," she replied.

"I see. And you're aware of what they did?"

"I know they were caught vandalizing school property?"

"That was only their most recent offense," she explained. "Before that, they were on probation for . . . hold on, let me see." She put on a pair of glasses, removed a sheet of paper from a folder in the desk's top drawer, and began to read from it. "Setting a trash can on fire, setting a classmate's shoes on fire, kidnapping half a dozen frogs from the science lab and setting them free two days later in the quad, getting caught with illegal substances, spray painting obscenities on their own lockers, stealing test answers from a math teacher's desk, giving another student a stick-and-poke tattoo during class, and last but not least, multiple altercations of a physical nature with both other students and faculty members."

"I see," Darcy said, shocked at the scope of the damage Kit and Lyle had done. "And this is all *both* of them?"

"Yep," said Dawn. "When one of them gets into trouble of any kind, they both insist on taking responsibility. They won't let each other go down alone."

"Well, that's . . . sweet," said Darcy.

"Sure, that's one word for it. I would have gone with something more like *demented* or *concerning,* but sure, *sweet* works too."

"But they're just boys," Darcy said, trying her best to brush off their behavior, which was, in fact, concerning. "They're just acting out. It's a phase."

"No, dying your hair is a phase, smoking cigarettes is a phase. These offenses are the beginnings of genuinely criminal behavior."

"Oh, I don't know about that. Look, I've known these boys since they were—"

"What exactly can I help you with, Darcy?" Dawn interrupted, looking at the clock behind Darcy's head.

"Well, like I was saying, I've known these kids practically their whole lives, and it would break my heart in a million pieces if they were sent away to juvenile hall. They wouldn't recover from it; their futures would be ruined. Statistics show that most kids come out of there more troubled than when they went in, and how could they not? It's practically torture in there. From what I've read, I do believe those kids are treated inhumanely, and I can't let Kit and Lyle end up there. They're like nephews to me."

"Darcy," insisted Mrs. Walsh, "we don't know what else to do with them. They can't keep going to school here—they've caused too much trouble. And no other school will take them— their reputations are way too tarnished. They've caused thousands of dollars of damage at Pemberley High, not to mention the psychological damage inflicted on many of the students."

"Okay, fair," said Darcy, chewing on her lip. "But what if I were to pay you for all the damage they've done?"

"Yeah, what if?" Mrs. Walsh sounded simultaneously annoyed and intrigued, prompting Darcy to go on.

"Would you agree not to send them to juvie?"

"Well, no, because even if you paid for all the damage they've done, that won't prevent them from causing further damage in the future, now will it?"

"What if I paid for all of it," she blurted out, surprising herself. "You can bill me."

"I'm sorry, who are you, again?"

"I'm just . . . I'm just somebody trying to do the right thing."

"And you're willing to pay for everything? How could you possibly have enough money for that?"

"I just do. And I'd love it if you'd considered my offer."

"I'm considering it," she said, confusedly. "But to be honest, I really think these kids need some serious help. I think you're right, juvenile hall isn't the answer. That will only damage them further. But in addition to you . . . *paying* for the property they destroy, I need their parents to enroll them in therapy. And I'll need weekly signatures from their therapists."

"Deal!" Darcy exclaimed. "Oh my goodness, Mrs. Walsh, you're doing an incredible thing right now. I don't know if you can tell that yet, but this really, really is right."

"I agree; that's why I'm doing it," said Mrs. Walsh, still looking at Darcy like a mythical being that had come gallivanting into her office. "But the other parents at the school, they won't like this. Nobody wants these delinquents around anymore. They're all going to need a lot of convincing."

"Do you have a phone list?" asked Darcy, with a sly smile.

"Um . . . yes."

"Then I'll take care of it."

"Where have you been?" Bingley asked, as Darcy came flying through the door to his parents' house. "I've been waiting for you for almost an hour."

"I had to do something important. I'm sorry, I should have texted." She plopped down on the couch and let her head fall back. "Bingley, being a good person is exhausting."

"Uh . . ." Bingley sat down next to her. "Wanna tell me what happened?"

"Yes," said Darcy, lifting her head back up. "But you can't tell anyone what I did."

"Wait, let me get this straight. You did something . . . *good* . . . but you don't want anyone to know?"

"Yeah. I wanna be humble about it or whatever."

"You, my dear," Bingley said, laughing, "are a character. All right, let's hear about this good deed."

"I went to Pemberley High and spoke to the new principal, Mrs. Walsh, and I told her I couldn't let Kit and Lyle go to juvenile hall, and I offered to pay for all the damage they've caused, and she said that wasn't good enough, so I said I'd pay for any future damages as well, so . . ." She took a deep breath. "She agreed to let them stay at Pemberley."

"What?" Bingley stared, dumbfounded. "Are you out of your mind?"

"Well, yes, probably, but in a good way, right?"

"I mean, in a very good way. The Bennets are going to be so relieved. Oh my God, you have to tell them that it was you. They'll love you forever."

"No. I told you, I need to practice being humble. Doing things for others without taking the credit."

"Fine." Bingley rolled his eyes. "If you insist. But wait, those kids are literal nightmares. You could end up paying thousands of dollars a month." He laughed at the thought of this.

"So? Guess how much I make in a month."

"Honestly," said Bingley, "I don't even want to know."

"It's not a big deal. And besides, it's worth it if I can keep them out of that horrible detention center."

"Don't you think maybe they need . . . professional help?"

"Oh, they definitely do. Mrs. Walsh will require them to go to weekly therapy sessions."

"Don't tell me you're—"

"Paying for that too? Yeah."

"Incredible."

"Feels good to be good," said Darcy. "I think I like it. Okay, so what else is new in Pemberley?"

"Well . . ." Bingley winced. "I don't really want to tell you."

"Well, you have to," Darcy said, feeling her pulse quicken. Her very least favorite thing in life was having secrets kept from her.

"Okay," he said hesitantly, "I'm just going to say it. Luke and Charlotte decided to majorly speed up their wedding process."

"Oh?" Darcy blinked, taking this in. "How majorly?"

"The rehearsal dinner is tonight." Bingley winced again. "The wedding is tomorrow."

"But . . . it's . . . they're having a rehearsal dinner on Christmas?"

"Yeah. I know. See why I didn't want to tell you?"

"Well, that's fine." Darcy tried to brush it off. "What do I care? It's not like Luke is my ex-boyfriend or anything like that. Luke and I never even *happened*. I don't even *like* Luke. Why should I care if he gets married?"

"I know about how you showed up at his house, and what you said to him."

"What? I didn't say anything. I don't know what you're talking about." She tried hard to make this sound convincing but could sense that she had failed miserably.

"Darcy."

"Ug-g-gh, are you serious?" She hid her head in her hands. "Luke told you about it? This is so embarrassing."

"No, Jim told me. He was there, remember?"

"Oh yeah."

"Darcy, you shouldn't feel embarrassed. It was a last-ditch effort at love. No one can blame you for that."

"Well, Luke did. He called me a self-obsessed snob who thinks she's better than everyone else. He said someone like me doesn't even know what love is."

"Ouch," said Bingley. "Jim didn't tell me that part."

"He probably didn't hear it."

"I'm sorry, Darcy."

"I'll survive. At least I'm not marrying someone who's totally wrong for me. That was a close one."

"Indeed," said Bingley. "How are you going to tell your parents?"

"Oh God, Bingley, I have no idea. They're going to murder me. But the way news travels in this town, I wouldn't be surprised if they already know. Carl's parents have probably told them."

"Maybe," Bingley agreed. "But don't you think they'd have called you by now?"

"Probably true. But either way, they'll find out soon enough, and then I'm basically dead. Oh God, I'm going to be excommunicated from my family for the second time. Dammit, I had just *finally* gotten onto the right foot with them."

"If your relationship with them could recover from that, then it can recover from this too, don't you think?"

"I have no idea. And in the meantime, what am I supposed to do? All I can think of is getting a room at the nearest hotel and hiding there for the rest of my life. What do you think about that?"

"I . . . I think it's a start."

Darcy entertained the idea in her mind. It occurred to her that she didn't want to go back to work, that with the fear of her father's wrath and the crushing blow of losing Luke and Carl in just a few days' time, she had little interest in actually doing anything. This was yet another new feeling, not wanting to go to work. Until this moment, work had been her very favorite thing, her saving grace. Now, suddenly, work didn't seem to matter. Actually, nothing seemed to matter. All she wanted to do was curl up in bed and stay there forever.

"Oh my God, Bingley." She grabbed his hand and held tight. "I think my throat is closing up. I can't swallow. What's happening?" She inhaled deeply, struggling to fill her lungs with air.

"What do you mean? Can you breathe?"

"I don't know. No, I can't breathe."

"I once read that if you can talk it means you can breathe. So if you stop being able to talk, that's when we have a problem."

"Am I having a heart attack?" She thought of her mother and how these ran in her family, especially among the stressed and overworked, which her mother was not, though Darcy definitely was.

"How are your arms?"

"My *arms*? Fine."

"Then you're not having a heart attack. Darcy, you're hyper-ventilating. I think this is a panic attack. You're going to be okay. Take slow breaths. In . . . out . . . in . . ."

She followed his lead until her heartbeat relaxed and she felt her throat loosening up.

"What the hell was that, Bingley?" she snapped, terrified of whatever force had just descended upon her.

"It's just intense anxiety. It feels like you're dying, but you're not."

"That was literally the worst. I don't understand where it came from."

"Darcy," he said lovingly, "you have a lot of stressors right now. You're beyond overwhelmed. It would be crazy if you didn't have a panic attack during all this. You broke off an en-gagement, your relationship with your family is at stake, Luke said some really unkind things about you, you just agreed to pay potentially tens of thousands of dollars so some kids you don't even know don't go to juvie—for some odd reason that I still don't really understand, unless maybe you're having a manic episode. All of this is really distressing stuff, Darcy. I think you need to take it easy. Don't get a hotel room; just stay right here. I'll set you up in the guest room, okay?"

"Okay," she agreed weakly, relieved by the idea of not hav-ing to go anywhere or do anything.

"You just stay here. I'll be right back," Bingley said, pulling a throw blanket up around her. Darcy nodded and closed her eyes. She took a deep breath and realized that she was thirsty. *When was the last time I had something to drink?* she wondered, unable to come up with the answer. She thought to ask Bingley for a glass of water, but he was already down the hall, and after all he was doing for her, she didn't want to impose any further.

She shuffled the blanket off her shoulders and stood up off the couch, feeling a little bit wobbly and light-headed. She took a few steps toward the kitchen before the room began to spin around her. Before she knew what was happening, everything went dark, and the last thing she remembered was the sound of her head hitting the coffee table with a thud.

17

Darcy woke in a blue hospital gown, looking down at her bare feet. She wiggled her toes, sending blood swirling through them. In a confused daze, she moved her attention to her arms and legs, lightly shaking them just to make sure they could move. *What happened to me?* she wondered. *And how did I end up here?*

She tried to remember the events leading up to now, but all she could think of was standing up to get water at Bingley's house. *That's right,* she thought, *I was with Bingley. And I thought I was dying. And he said it wasn't a heart attack. And then I stood up and everything went dark.* She let her eyelids fall back shut so she could think more clearly. *Bingley must have been wrong,* she surmised. *It actually* was *a heart attack.* This realization didn't bring her any solace but instead sent her heart back into a flurry. *Am I going to die?* she wondered, snapping her eyes back open and looking frantically around the room.

For a hospital, it was quite a lovely room. It had a flat-screen TV, periwinkle curtains with white honeysuckle blossoms, and a big whiteboard to her left, with what looked like red squiggly marks jotted all over it. She blinked her eyes into focus and saw that the marks were actually words. They read "DARCY FITZWILLIAM, AGE 29, FEMALE, DEHYDRATION."

The word *dehydration* rang out like a comforting bell in her mind.

Oh thank God, she sighed, placing her hand over her heart, so relieved to know that nothing was wrong with it. At first she was so relieved that she laughed, letting go of all the worry that had her so tightly seized up. But then less laughable thoughts came creeping in. *This is embarrassing,* she realized. *I'm in the hospital for forgetting to drink enough water? I'll be the laughingstock of the town.* But soon something much more serious occurred to her: if she was in the hospital in a town as tiny as Pemberley, Ohio, her parents would definitely have been notified by now and would know that she was back in town.

"Dammit," she cursed out loud. "I have to get out of here." She tried to stand up but realized she was too woozy to lift her head, let alone her whole body. It was then that she noticed the IV tube stuck in her right arm. Even if she could manage to get out of bed, she wasn't crazy or desperate enough to rip an IV out of her arm, so there was officially nowhere she could go. She pressed the shiny red button on the left of her bed, hoping she could get a nurse to take pity on her and get her out of there before anyone could find her.

She felt dumb for coming back to Pemberley. She had left New York to avoid Carl and give him space, but why'd she have to come back here, walking right into the lion's den that was her family's hometown? Why couldn't she have gone to Europe? Asia? Hawaii? Why couldn't she have gone literally anywhere else but here? She suspected the answer had something to do with Luke, and she wasn't happy about it.

A handsome nurse strode energetically into the room.

"Knock, knock," he said, in lieu of actually knocking. "How are we feeling, Ms. Fitzwilliam?"

"Fine," she lied. "Absolutely fine. I think I'm ready to go home now."

The nurse laughed, checking the IV bag and making a note on the whiteboard.

"You can't go home yet, Ms. Fitzwilliam. You fainted from dehydration. We can't let you out until your levels are back to normal."

"Listen," she tried to reason, "I'm a very healthy person. And I really can't be here right now. Once my parents realize I'm here, they'll come find me, and my father is going to kill me. Not literally kill me, but he is going to throw a fit so rageful we will all wish we had never been born, do you understand? You have to let me out; it's what's best for both of us."

"But Ms. Fitzwilliam . . . I don't know how to tell you this, but your parents are already here. They're in the waiting room."

"*Excuse me?*" Darcy felt as though she might throw up. "Why are they here? Who told them?"

"Ms. Fitzwilliam, it's fine. They don't seem mad at all."

"Well, obviously! They're not going to be mad at *you*! Do you know who told them I was here?"

"I don't . . . but they're with a good-looking man who may or may not be Darren Criss."

"That's Bingley. And trust me, as handsome as he is, you do not want to date him. He looks sweet, but apparently he's a backstabber. Send him in. Please."

"And your parents too?"

"Dear Lord, no. Just the handsome backstabber."

"Right." The nurse gave an exasperated sigh and left the room. Soon after, Bingley stepped in and closed the door quietly behind him.

"You look better," he said, clearly bracing himself.

"*What the hell, Bingley?*"

"What? What did I do?" he demanded defensively. "What was I supposed to do, huh? Not take you to the hospital after you collapsed and hit your head on my coffee table? Not call your parents to let them know what had happened?"

"Correct. You could have taken me here without telling them. You know I can't handle seeing them now, especially in such a vulnerable condition."

"I was scared, Darcy. Put yourself in my shoes. You hit your head and weren't responsive. I couldn't, in good conscience, not tell your parents."

"Oh," said Darcy, reeling herself back in. "I wasn't responsive?"

"No, you weren't. It was really scary. I called nine-one-one and everything. They sent an ambulance. I had to let your parents know what had happened. I just kept thinking 'What if she dies and I'm the one who didn't tell the Fitzwilliams she hit her head?,' and I kept worrying that this whole thing was somehow my fault, maybe I shouldn't have—"

"No, no, no, Bingley, it's okay," Darcy interrupted. "I'm not mad. And I'm sorry I yelled at you; that was wrong of me. I didn't realize the extent of what had happened. And even if I hadn't hit my head and an ambulance hadn't come, you were just trying to do what you thought was right. It's not your fault I'm avoiding my parents anyway."

"Apology accepted. But Darcy, just so you know, they really don't seem mad. They're relieved that you're okay, and they really want to see you."

"Then they don't know about Carl yet. If they're not mad, they don't know."

"Well then, maybe now is the right time to tell them."

"Now?" The shrillness in Darcy's voice came barreling back. "So that I can have another heart attack?"

"Darcy," he laughed, "you didn't have a heart attack."

"No, but I will if I have to tell them what happened with Carl and see the look on my dad's face. Look, just send them in. I don't want to keep them worrying."

"You'll be fine," said Bingley, squeezing her foot affectionately. He stepped out into the hall and was quickly replaced by Mr. and Mrs. Fitzwilliam, who rushed in practically gasping for breath. In all the time she'd known her parents, she had never seen them move so quickly.

"Thank God you're all right!" said Mrs. Fitzwilliam, hurrying to her daughter's side.

"Jesus Christ," said Mr. Fitzwilliam, sighing with relief. "Will you two please stop getting yourselves into hospitals? I'm too old for this stress."

"I'm fine, Dad." Darcy smiled sweetly up at him. "It was just a little dehydration."

"But you might have a concussion too," her mom reminded her. "They're still doing tests."

"Okay, but still, I'm going to survive. Nothing serious. I'll be good as new in no time. Mom survived a heart attack, so I'm sure this won't set me back much."

"Sweetheart," Mr. Fitzwilliam said gently, taking a seat at the foot of the bed. "We know about what happened."

"What are you talking about?"

"We know that you broke things off with Carl," explained Mrs. Fitzwilliam.

"*You do?*" Darcy couldn't understand. If they knew about Carl, why weren't they furious? Why weren't they yelling?

"Yes," said Mrs. Fitzwilliam. "And we aren't mad."

"Well," Mr. Fitzwilliam chuckled, "we were confused. But when Bingley called to tell us that you had hit your head and weren't responsive, well, that put things in perspective."

"Oh." Darcy spoke slowly, as if walking through a minefield, afraid she might accidentally set off a bomb at any moment. "Well, I—"

"Listen, Darcy," Mr. Fitzwilliam interrupted. "You don't have to explain yourself. I think I'm the one who needs to explain." He pulled up a chair and sat down so that he and Darcy were eye to eye. "And maybe to apologize."

"Oh?"

"It was devastating when you left home, Darcy. I don't know

how I let it catch me off guard, but it did. The thing is, that I need to take responsibility for"—he looked back at his wife, who nodded encouragingly for him to go on—"is that I made it about Carl when it really just . . . well, it wasn't."

"It wasn't . . . about Carl?"

"No. Don't get me wrong. Carl is a nice young man and comes from an excellent family, but the real reason I was so gung ho on you marrying him was because it would mean you'd stay close to home and we, or, well, *I* wouldn't lose you."

"But so . . . all you ever really wanted was for me to stay in Pemberley?"

"You're my only daughter, and by far the smartest and most delightful of all my children. Sorry, but it's true."

"No need to apologize for *that*." Darcy smiled slyly.

"I wanted you by my side, my little co-captain, like when you were growing up."

"But . . . I thought . . . I thought this was about marrying into the Donovan family. You wanted me to marry up and make us look good. It all just felt so . . . contrived. I had to get away from . . . I had to go somewhere where nobody else had a say over how I lived my life."

"And I understand that now. I just wish you knew you could have had total say over your life without leaving Pemberley. I never wanted to control you; I just wanted you to be close to home."

"But . . . when I left, you turned your back on me. Why would you risk not seeing me at all if the whole point was you wanted to see more of me?"

"It really hurt me when you left. I had big plans for you. I wanted you to help me run the company. I took it personally that you wanted to leave, and that was petty. I thought, somehow, freezing you out would make you change your mind and come home. I see now how that backfired. In retrospect, my behavior seems ridiculous, to be honest."

"It was," said Darcy. "But I think I probably would have done the same thing. I'm stubborn, and I get that from you."

"That's true," he nodded, grateful for her magnanimity.

"This is just so odd." She looked around, feeling dazed. "All these years, I thought you hated me for not marrying Carl, and that made me so mad."

"Honey, I never hated you. Never in a million years."

"But if I'd known this wasn't about Carl, but just about you . . . liking me so much that you wanted me close . . . well, I wouldn't have been so spiteful."

"Well, then, this has all been a very unfortunate misunderstanding," he said, patting her hand. "And I'm sorry." She could tell these last few words were a strain for him, but she appreciated his intention.

Darcy didn't know what to say. Nobody had ever said anything like this to her. Be who you want to be? Do what you want to do? No pressure? She didn't know what to do with this information, so she let it percolate in her mind, bubbling wildly, as she stared in disbelief at her mom and dad.

"So you . . . do you mean that?"

"Yes, of course," said Mrs. Fitzwilliam. "We don't want you to do anything you don't want to do. We'll love you no matter what. Isn't that right, dear?" She turned to her husband with an urging glance, eyebrows raised insistently.

"That's right."

"But . . ." Darcy said, remembering, "you said if I didn't

marry Carl you'd cut me off financially. It was so important to you."

"I panicked! You were going to leave home and I panicked. We were so close for so long, Darcy, and I couldn't handle the thought of you running around New York City with all those Wall Street scoundrels and rats and . . . *subways*." He grimaced. Darcy laughed.

"Dad, I'm a millionaire. I don't *take* the subway."

"It was ignorant of me . . . and unfair to try to keep you from spreading your wings. Just know I did it out of fear. But the truth is . . . you've never let anyone tell you how to live your life, and *that's* what I'm most proud of."

"Very good, dear." Mrs. Fitzwilliam patted her husband's shoulder approvingly. "That was perfect."

Darcy burst into tears. She didn't try to stop herself, or even want to try to stop herself. She cried from the relief of knowing, for the first time, that she was loved unconditionally; she cried for the loss of Carl and the frustration of Luke; she cried for all the years she'd cursed herself for letting down her family, all that time wasted in secret self-loathing; and last, she cried tears of joy from knowing she'd never have to live like that again.

"Angel, what's wrong?" asked Mrs. Fitzwilliam. Mr. Fitzwilliam shifted uncomfortably, apparently not used to seeing people cry.

"Nothing's wrong." Darcy laughed through her tears. "I'm just really happy. I'm happy this is all over. I'm happy to be home with my family."

"Maybe you should . . ." Mr. Fitzwilliam looked to his wife for approval. She nodded for him to go ahead. "Maybe you should

move back home for a little while. Just to take a break and relax. You can have as much space as you need. We can give you
the entire guesthouse; you'll never even see us."

"Dad!" Darcy laughed. "But I would want to see you."

"You would?"

"Yes. And I think you make a good point. I'm going to think
about it." Darcy meant what she said. What was there for her in
New York anymore? She had virtually no social life to speak of,
and she was financially set for life. She'd been working so hard
for so many years, out of the need to prove herself. She'd been
driven by wanting to run away from the past, but now she felt
she neither had to prove herself nor run away from the past.

18

Cozy and content, Darcy sat up in her childhood bed, watching *Gilmore Girls* and eating rocky road ice cream directly out of the carton. In her mind she was practicing how she would tell her partners that she was cashing out from Montrose Montrose and Fitzwilliam, and to her surprise, none of it made her anxious at all. She'd made more than enough to last them and future generations for a good long while—that was one of the benefits of being partner. The sun was setting on Christmas Day and, though she was spending it alone, she felt wildly grateful to have her health, the love of her family, and her few but close friends, namely Bingley.

Just then, there was a knock at the door.

"Uh, who is it?" she asked. After Darcy had convinced everyone that she was feeling much better, her parents went out to a cocktail party and, as far as she knew, her brothers were with their significant others.

"It's Bingley."

"Bingley? What are you doing here?"

"Can I come in?" he asked through the door. Darcy laughed.

"Yes, yes, get in here."

Bingley came in and sat at the foot of her bed. He was wearing a white dress shirt buttoned to his neck, with a navy silk tie, and she could smell expensive cologne wafting off of him.

"How are you feeling?" he asked.

"Amazing, actually. How are you? You look fancy. Where are you going?"

"The rehearsal dinner," he said delicately. "For Luke and Charlotte."

"Oh, right," Darcy grumbled. "I forgot that was tonight."

"You didn't forget."

"Nope."

"I think you should come with me."

"*Ha!*" Darcy guffawed. "Yeah, right. Why the hell would I volunteer to embarrass myself like that?"

"I don't think it would be embarrassing. I think it would show that you're thinking about people other than yourself. I know you wanted to do that by helping out Kit and Lyle, but nobody's gonna know you did that."

"Hmm." She thought it over. "But it's not like I was invited."

"Actually, you were. Your parents didn't give you the invitation at the hospital because the doctor said not to do anything to agitate you."

"Oh. But still, I wouldn't want my presence to be any kind of distraction to him on this night. The night before your wedding should be a drama-free night."

"Wow," said Bingley. "You really are starting to think about people other than yourself."

"Yeah," she said. "I guess I really am."

"I'm just a text away if you need me."

"Thanks, Bingley, you're the best."

"I'll stop by after, to check up on you."

"I can't wait."

"Love ya," he said, opening the door.

"Love ya too," she replied, as he shut the door behind him.

An hour later the wheels in Darcy's mind started to turn. They started to turn faster and faster, until she had to hit Pause on *Gilmore Girls* because she couldn't focus on their quick and witty dialogue.

Why would Luke invite me to his rehearsal dinner? she wondered. *Why would he do that if he thinks I'm a brat and a snob? Did he do it to prove that I think I'm better than everybody else? Everyone would show up except me, and then it would be obvious that I can't show up for anybody unless it benefits me? What a jerk. I'm not a snob, and I do care about other people. I'm a grown-ass woman and I can show up for my lifelong classmate and neighbor, show my support, even if he said all those things about me. I'll show up and I'll be gracious and that will show him. Luke Bennet, get ready to meet the new Darcy Fitzwilliam.*

She hopped out of bed and opened her closet. She picked the first dress she saw off its hanger and pulled it over her head.

She didn't have a lot of time, she knew, to arrive on time without making a scene, and it didn't matter what she looked like if she was going to make this night as not about her as possible. She was going to blend in, in this taupe, conservatively styled dress, and she wouldn't have it any other way.

Bingley will be proud of me, she thought, stepping into a pair of brown leather kitten heels. *I'm being very grown up about this. Sure, I wanted Luke, but things didn't work out that way. A brat would throw a fit, but I am not a brat. I am a magnanimous and compassionate lady, and I do not hold grudges.*

She bundled up, preparing for the cold, and called an Uber. She tapped her foot nervously the whole ride to the venue, worried she'd be late and that her lateness would be misunderstood as an intentional slight. She hoped when she arrived she could slip in among the crowd, find Bingley as soon as possible, and latch on to him for the night.

But when she hurried up the front steps and opened the restaurant door, the place was completely empty and the lights were turned down so low they were practically off. *Oh my God, I missed it entirely,* she thought. *Or, wait, maybe I got the address wrong?*

"How could I have gotten the address wrong?" she said out loud, cursing herself.

"You didn't," said a voice in the dark, startling Darcy. She recognized that voice; it was Luke's.

"Luke?" she asked, baffled. He stood up and into the beam of light cast by an outside streetlamp.

"Hi, Darcy," he said humbly, arms crossed over his chest.

"What happened to the rehearsal dinner?"

"There's no dinner," he said. "I called it off. Actually, I called the wedding off, the whole thing."

"But . . . why?"

"It was the hardest thing I've ever had to do, but I realized Charlotte wasn't the right girl for me. I thought she was, but she wasn't."

"What made you realize that?" Darcy looked down at her shoes.

"You."

"*Me?*" Her eyes grew big with acute curiosity. "But I thought I'm—"

"Darcy, I am so sorry for what I said to you that day. It was horrible of me, and I can't take it back, but I can tell you how sorry I am."

"I don't understand. How did you . . . What made you . . ."

"Mrs. Walsh from Pemberley High called me. She told me what you did. Honestly, it blew me away. That you would do that for my family . . . it was just incredible of you. And then, on top of that, you didn't even tell me? You truly did it just to help. It made me realize how wrong I was about you, Darcy, wrong from the beginning. I judged you because of your money and your privilege, but that was so immature of me. You're not a snob; you're just different than I am. Different in a good way. You have ambition and drive and I . . . I think I love you for that. You're a wonderful girl, Darcy, and I was an idiot to push you away. Please forgive me."

Darcy felt the blood drain from her head, and for a second she thought she might pass out again. She blinked repeatedly, trying to wake herself up from what surely had to be a dream. But she wasn't waking up, because this wasn't a dream. The restaurant was real and Luke standing there was real and all the things he had just said were real. She took a deep breath, knowing her life would never be the same after this moment.

"I forgive you, Luke," she said, taking a step toward him. "And I love you too."

He rushed to her then, lifted her by her waist, and spun her around so that her taupe-colored dress swooshed and swirled.

"I'm so happy," he said. "You're incredible."

She beamed giddily and looked up at the ceiling.

"There's no mistletoe," she said.

"Oh man," he said. "That's too bad. I guess we just have to go home."

"All right then," she joked, pretending to leave. "See ya later."

Luke grabbed her wrist and pulled her close to him. He pressed his lips eagerly up against hers, and they stood there together, just like that, as the snow outside came down all around them, falling perfectly into place.

Darcy could remember every single Christmas since the time she was three years old. Not many people have memories from that far back, but Darcy did, and was mostly proud of that fact. The Christmas she was three she sat at the base of the gilded tree as her brother Kenneth tore the gift wrap off box after box and threw it into piles that built around her until she was in a sea of shiny, glossy paper shreds.

In later years, once James was born, a tradition developed among them of leaving cookies out for Santa Claus, next to a potted plant in the upstairs hallway. They'd stay awake for as long as possible, peeking under the cracks beneath their doors, hoping to catch a glimpse of him as he stopped for his nighttime snack. But Darcy never bothered to stay awake. She curled into bed early each Christmas Eve and shut out her light, because even at eight years old there wasn't a shadow of a doubt in her mind that Santa Claus was a big, sad, pathetic lie. She couldn't believe how dumb her brothers were for falling for such a hoax—especially Kenneth, who was older than she was and *definitely* should have known better.

The simple logistical errors in the myth of Santa Claus seemed so obvious to her. He was one man who had an entire planet's worth of presents to give out in the span of twenty-four hours—did nobody else care to comment on the sheer impossibility of this? Not to mention the flying sleigh, which was just straight up not a thing that existed. You'd have to throw out logic and believe in magic in order to buy this story, which she did not.

Then there was the issue of naughtiness versus niceness. The adults wanted you to believe that the amount of presents you received on Christmas morning had to do with how well behaved you were throughout the year. This was how they got you to follow rules, an obvious ploy in Darcy's mind. The truth, she observed in the school days following Christmas, was that the amount of gifts you received on Christmas had nothing to do with how you behaved and everything to do with how much money your parents had. This realization in itself debunked the Santa myth on its own, because if there really was a Santa Claus, who was supposedly a benevolent monitor of childhood morality, he would never let this happen; he would make sure well-behaved children got good presents no matter how poor they were. He would go straight to third world countries, where the kids were hungry and courageous, and he would make sure to give them food before flying over to Ohio to make sure all the brats Darcy went to school with got their My Size Barbies and their Furbies and their Kid Motorz Hummers. But there were kids who were starving to death all over the world—this much she overheard on morning talk radio that Edward listened to—and so there couldn't possibly be a Santa Claus. And on that note, she figured, there probably wasn't a God either.

Those were Darcy's childhood Christmases.

As a teenager, once the Santa dream was squashed for her naive and gullible siblings, the Christmas tradition morphed into the Fitzwilliam parents asking the Fitzwilliam kids point blank what they would like for Christmas, and then delivering. She knew her parents most likely did not look at the list but instead passed it over to one of their many assistants to take care of. Either way, the excitement of seeing who got what presents was nonexistent, so Darcy chose to sleep in. Why wake at the crack of dawn to open presents she already knew she was getting and that would be waiting there for her all day?

Furthermore, once she turned fourteen, she only ever asked for various books, and those she definitely didn't have to wake up early for. Some of her favorites that she asked for and received over the years were *The Intelligent Investor* by Benjamin Graham, *Think and Grow Rich* by Napoleon Hill, *Common Sense on Mutual Funds* by John C. Bogle, *One Up on Wall Street* by Peter Lynch, and *Reminiscences of a Stock Operator*. The year she was sixteen she got into the biographies of the billionaires she admired most: John D. Rockefeller and Andrew Carnegie and Cornelius Vanderbilt. The year she was seventeen she grew frustrated with and bored of reading about rich men and began seeking out the rich women she could learn from. Research at the Pemberley High library led her to Geraldine Weiss, Debra Cafaro, and Susan Shaw. It was around this time that she became appalled at how few women were successful or acknowledged in the world of stocks, and she decided that, when she grew up, she'd aspire to do something about it.

After almost an hour of kissing Luke in the snow, she forced herself to break free from him to go home and celebrate what was left of Christmas with her family. Having not returned to Pemberley for eight years, she had gone eight years without providing a list for her parents. And not having prepared to be in Pemberley this year and therefore not providing her parents with a list of requests (because why would she?), she was not expecting any gifts. But on this Christmas night, Darcy made her way through the front door and into the downstairs living room to find an obscene display of professionally wrapped presents beneath the oversize tree, and her entire family lounging casually on the living room furniture, each one looking lazier and merrier than the last.

"There she is!" said Kenneth. "Late to Christmas as usual."

"Why haven't you opened the presents yet?" she asked.

"We opened ours already," James explained. "These ones are for you."

"*These?*" Darcy stared in shock at the bounty. These couldn't possibly all be for her. She wasn't even expecting one present, let alone what looked like about fifty.

"Yes," Mrs. Fitzwilliam laughed. "What, did you think we'd forget about you?"

"No, I uh . . ." Darcy tried to find the right words. "I just thought since you didn't know I was coming home you wouldn't have time to get me anything."

"Wouldn't have enough time?" Mrs. Fitzwilliam laughed. "Please, darling, though you just got here, we work fast. We had time to prepare."

"But . . ." Darcy began breathlessly, staring at the gifts. "There are just so many of them. How did you . . . Why would you . . . When did you . . . Even as a kid I never got this many presents in one Christmas."

"Oh, these aren't for one Christmas," said Mr. Fitzwilliam. Darcy was confused.

"They're not?" she asked.

"These are all your presents accumulated over the past eight years, since you've been away from Pemberley," explained James. "You weren't coming home anymore, but we assumed you'd still want presents."

"*What?*" Darcy laughed incredulously. "I don't mean to sound disrespectful or unappreciative; I'm just trying to understand. Why didn't you just mail them to me?"

"If we mailed you your presents, then you'd really have no reason to ever come home," said Mrs. Fitzwilliam.

"Yeah," added William. "We wanted to make sure, whenever it was that you came home, you'd have a good reason to want to stay."

Darcy was baffled. She didn't know what to say. First of all, there was their serious gap in logic. Darcy was a multimillionaire and could buy herself anything her heart desired. She didn't need to come home to Pemberley, Ohio, in order to get gifts. Had she known presents were waiting for her, it would still be no motivation to fly home. Surely her family must have understood that. Second of all, if they wanted to lure her home with presents, why would they not tell her these presents existed? Third of all, and most important, she had no idea her family felt this way about her. She knew her mom was fond of her, but as far as she had known, her dad resented the hell out of her and her brothers were mostly irritated by her existence (most likely because they were intimidated by her, she told herself). How could she have been so completely wrong? She had fled and never looked back because she thought they wanted her gone, but could it be that, all along, they had wanted her here?

"This is . . . incredible. Incredibly sweet," she said, bringing one hand to her chest. "You really didn't have to do this."

"The Fitzwilliams don't have to do anything," Kenneth reminded her. "We wanted to do this."

"Even you?" she laughed.

"Yes, even me!" He laughed with her. "You're arrogant and irritating but you're my sister and I love you."

Whoa. The *L* word. Darcy hadn't heard that word from anyone in her family in years and years. Hearing it now, she was taken aback, and was surprised to find that she had to fight back tears.

"Welcome home, honey." Mrs. Fitzwilliam stood up from her reclined position to hug her daughter. "Grab a hot chocolate and start opening your presents!"

"Now?"

"Definitely now," said James. "What the hell else are we going to do on Christmas?"

"Oh, okay." She smiled hesitantly. "Sure, why not?"

Self-consciously, she sat down at the base of the tree and surveyed the boxes. She felt uncomfortable with her entire family's gaze on her. The pressure was on and the stakes felt high. She would have to like every gift, and when she didn't, she would have to pretend.

"Now, remember," her mom said, "we didn't have a list from you for eight whole years, so we had to improvise. We hope you like them, but we won't be offended if you don't."

"Oh, okay." Darcy nodded, trying to hide her feelings of being overwhelmed.

She chose a box at random and began to slowly unwrap it.

"Ooh, I think this is the one from 2012," said James, looking to William. "Remember?"

"Ah yes," William replied. "She'll like this one, I bet."

Beneath the paper was a boxy, sleek black suitcase that looked like it could be made of alligator skin. There was a silver latch that read "Open me." She opened up the suitcase, and inside was the most stunning typewriter she had ever seen. It was polished, glossy black with pearl keys, each one a perfect circle. *They're much nicer to look at than the square keys of computers,* she thought.

"It's a 1920s Smith Corona," Mr. Fitzwilliam said. "It belonged to Napoleon Hill."

"I'm sorry, *what*?" Darcy stared.

"You heard him correctly, sweetie," Mrs. Fitzwilliam assured her.

"How did you find it?" she marveled.

"It was at a Sotheby's auction in London," her dad explained. "And I remembered how you always were a fan of him and his work. So I made sure I was the highest bidder."

"This is incredible!" She ran her fingers over the cool black metal.

"Oh, it wasn't that big of a deal," Mr. Fitzwilliam insisted. "It was easy. Nobody likes to try to bid against me because they know I always win."

"Well, thanks, Dad. I love it."

"Thought you might." He smiled briefly, then reverted back to his notoriously solemn resting face, as if to say, *Don't make this a sentimental moment.* Darcy was relieved, as she also was stubbornly against sentimental moments, or sentimentality of any kind at all.

"Open this one next," said Mrs. Fitzwilliam, rummaging through the boxes and producing a small rectangular one. "It's from 2010. It will be funny."

Still stunned and speechless from the typewriter, Darcy peeled off the old wrapping paper, which seemed to have almost permanently merged with the box beneath it.

"Oh my God, it's an iPod!" Darcy laughed nostalgically at the picture on the box of a silvery iPod with a white click wheel.

"Open up the box," said James. "Look what's inside."

Darcy opened the box.

"It's an iPod," she repeated, taking the iPod out of the box, not entirely sure what the point of it was. "Thanks so much, guys! What a time warp."

"Turn it on, turn it on!" William urged.

Despite it being eight years since she'd operated an iPod, her motor memory kicked in and she knew to slide the switch on the upper right corner in order to turn it on. The dark-gray screen flickered to life with a blushing white glow, and black digitalized letters appeared: the names of bands and songwriters and musicians of all kinds, in alphabetical order. Not just *any* musicians, but her *favorite* musicians at the time of 2010, to be specific: Ludwig van Beethoven and David Bowie and the Cure and George Gershwin and Philip Glass and Carole King and Joni Mitchell and Mozart and the Police and Carly Simon and the Rolling Stones. The list went on and on and on.

Wow, she thought, scrolling through, *they really must have been paying much closer attention to me than I ever thought.* She was pleased to see that, despite knowing her better than she thought, they still didn't know her guilty pleasures, which she always made a point of keeping secret: Taylor Swift and Britney Spears and Carly Rae Jepsen and Maroon 5 and even, sometimes, as ashamed as she was to admit it, Nickelback. She'd rather die than have anyone find out that she listened to any of these musical "talents." Truthfully, she found some of these to be genuinely talented (if she were a less prideful person, she'd defend Taylor and Britney to the bitter end), but so much of the power she held at work and around just about everyone in her life had to do with a carefully constructed appearance of toughness and transcendent, untouchable coolness.

"You guys . . . these are amazing presents," she told them. "I feel bad I didn't get anything for any of you. I just never thought—"

"Oh, you don't have to get us anything. That's not how it works," Mrs. Fitzwilliam explained. "The kids don't get the grown-ups presents. The grown-ups get the kids presents. Everyone knows that."

"Aren't we all grown-ups now?" William asked.

"You are *definitely* not a grown-up," James laughed.

"Oh, like you are?" Kenneth rolled his eyes.

"You'll all always be my babies," said Mrs. Fitzwilliam. "And a mother couldn't ask for better babies! You all came right over to see me when I had my heart attack. I'm just so grateful."

Mr. Fitzwilliam and Darcy recoiled at the mushy sentimentality of it all, then caught each other's eye and shared a knowing glance.

"Darcy, you gonna open the rest of your presents?" asked James. Darcy let her eyes rove over the remainder of the gifts and felt intimidated by them all.

"I think I need to take a break," she said. "Can I open the rest later?"

"Of course," said Mrs. Fitzwilliam. "They're your presents."

"Have some eggnog and chill," suggested Kenneth, lifting his porcelain mug. "That's what we're all doing."

"On Christmas you can start drinking whenever; everyone knows that," William reminded her. "It's like . . . it's like . . . it's like what?"

"An unspoken rule?" suggested James.

"Yes!" said William excitedly. "That's it!"

"Well, it's hard to argue with that," admitted Darcy. "One glass of the house eggnog, please."

Mrs. Fitzwilliam pulled a white porcelain mug from a stack of them and used a white porcelain pitcher to fill it with eggnog.

"Mm," said Darcy, bringing it to her lips. "Smells amazing." She took a sip and reclined deeply into the velvet armchair closest to the fireplace, feeling for the first time since she got back that she was actually home.

———

Later, the Fitzwilliams were still lounging, buzzed and lazy, around the fireplace. James got a phone call from his fiancée and Kenneth had fallen asleep with his head back and his tongue hanging out. William was drunkenly showing off his piano skills on the baby grand, playing a clumsy rendition of "Jingle Bell Rock."

"I think I'll bake my special Christmas chocolate chip cookies," Mrs. Fitzwilliam announced.

"Dr. Law said to avoid creams and butters, darling," Mr. Fitzwilliam reminded her, sitting upright in concern.

"Well, they're not for me," she said sassily, with her hands on her hips. "They're for my family."

"Well then," said Mr. Fitzwilliam, reclining back into his chair, "by all means. Be my guest."

"Thank you." Mrs. Fitzwilliam curtsied and exited dramatically into the kitchen.

Even though Darcy and her father had cleared the air that day, things between them still felt a little awkward.

"So, uh," he began, clearing his throat, "how are things in New York?"

"New York's great," she heard herself say. "Work is busy. I'll probably have to work crazy hours to make up for this vacation."

"I see."

"But, I mean, it's good." She realized how that could have come off as ungrateful, and she wanted to fix it. "I haven't had a vacation in three years and I'm really grateful to get one now."

"Well, it's no Bahamas, but at least it's something."

"It's more than something," she told him. "I'm actually really happy to be home."

"I thought you hated Pemberley."

"I don't hate Pemberley," she explained. "I actually love Pemberley. It's beautiful here. So many people I lo—like live here." She caught herself on the verge of the *L* word and reined herself in, not wanting to become any more vulnerable than she absolutely had to be right now. "I just don't want to live here. The world is so big; there's so much to see out there."

"I get that." He nodded. "Pemberley isn't exactly the thrill capital of the world."

"No," she laughed, "it's not."

"Look," he said. "I'm proud of all you're doing in New York. It's not easy making it on your own, let alone getting rich as hell on your own."

"*Really?*" She was shocked.

"Yes." He nodded. "You remind me of my mother. Her whole life she wanted to do things her own way, on her own conditions. She was headstrong and free-spirited, just like you."

"I thought I was selfish and entitled."

"You can be those things," he said with a sly smile. "But we all can be at times. We're Fitzwilliams. We were born entitled, unfortunately. It's a blessing and a curse, I suppose."

"I suppose so," she agreed.

"Look . . ." He took a deep breath. "You gotta understand, I wasn't trying to be an asshole by insisting you marry Carl. I was trying to do what I thought was best for you, and I wanted you to stay close to me. I thought it was best for you to have security and family and respect from the community and . . . you know, a life companion so you wouldn't have to go through life all alone." He shrugged, notably embarrassed. "But it turns out you didn't need a man to have security and respect from the community. You got that for yourself all on your own, and that's impressive. I was wrong. You're not the kind of girl who needs a man and a family to be happy. At least not now. And that's okay. I just wanted to let you know that I accept your path."

Darcy knew she should feel relieved. All she'd really wanted for the past eight years was for the guilt of letting down her family to be lifted from her shoulders. But she didn't feel relieved. Or pleased. Or comforted. Instead, she felt a cloud of sadness and worry begin to brew in her chest. She knew right away what it was: it was the words he'd used, words like *family* and *all alone* and *happy*. It was true, she had accomplished a lot, but this, she knew, was also true: she was all alone and she was not happy.

She blinked back her tears, wanting to let her dad know she appreciated what he had told her.

"Thank you, Dad," she said. "That really means a lot to me."

19

"You're honestly telling me that you didn't have a crush on me in high school?" Luke was lying underneath the blankets of Darcy's childhood bed while Darcy applied her lipstick, using a compact mirror, a charcoal-colored turtleneck pulled up snugly to her chin. It had been nearly twenty-four hours since their kiss, and Darcy's head still spun like a carousel.

"Yes, honestly." She laughed. "I thought you were . . . weird. Too rough around the edges." She wrinkled her nose.

"But you were always so . . . prickly with me. I could swear there was tension there."

"Yeah, the tension of me not liking you. What, are you honestly trying to tell me you thought I liked you back then?"

"Well, I liked you. And you were a jerk, but I always suspected it was because you were secretly into me."

"I was a jerk to you because you were a jerk to me!" she protested.

"And I was a jerk to you because I liked you! See my logic?"

"That's some pretty tangled logic, my friend."

"Nuh-uh." He pulled her close. "We're not just friends any-more."

"Oh really?" She set her mirror down and let herself be cajoled back into his arms. "What are we, then?"

"Well, let's see. I love you and you love me, even though you claim that you didn't have feelings for me in high school, which is probably a lie, and people who love each other shouldn't lie, so—"

He was interrupted by the pillow she used to whack him across the head.

"Stop being a moron," she giggled.

"Okay, okay." He composed himself in mock seriousness. "Would I . . . could I dare ask you, Darcy Fitzwilliam, to be my girlfriend?"

Girlfriend. The word sat like thick liquid in her stomach. She wondered why it made her so uncomfortable. First of all, there was the fact that she was almost thirty—was being a girlfriend taking a step back? She had been on the verge of being a wife, after all, hadn't she? Second of all, and buried deeper down, was the idea of a label that said she belonged to somebody—wife, fiancée, girlfriend, or otherwise—which had actively repelled her for as long as she could remember. Girlfriend, last time she checked, was just the first step you took that led to being chained to somebody for the rest of your life.

Darcy, get a grip, she told herself. *This is what you want, re-*

member? You want Luke; you fought for him. This is good. Be happy about this.

"Uh, Darcy?" he asked, snapping her out of this zooming train of thought. "Did you hear me?"

"Yes, of course." She blinked repeatedly. "And I'd love to be your girlfriend. I may not have liked you in high school, but I certainly made a point of letting my, uh . . . *current* feelings for you be known."

"I'd say so."

"So then we're officially boyfriend and girlfriend." She stood up out of bed and reached for a tan suede skirt that hung over the foot of the bed frame. "After all these years."

"Where are you going?" He pulled at her hand, trying to lure her back to bed.

"Well, we have to leave my room sometime. People are going to start to talk."

"Start to talk? They're already talking. We both called off engagements that the entire town knew about. I mean, I canceled my rehearsal dinner the night of."

"Still, I don't want my parents to think we're just in here . . . you know. The respectable thing would be to come out of hiding and, you know, acknowledge that things are different now. That I'm not getting married to Carl and you're not getting married to Charlotte and that . . . we're, you know, together now."

"Fine. But your dad is going to be pissed. I'm sure through his eyes you've majorly downgraded."

"Well, you're not his first choice for me, we can't deny that. But he just wants me to be happy. He'll see that you make me happy and then he'll be happy for me!"

"Let's hope so," Luke grumbled.

"Come on, get dressed. It's almost five. They'll be in the dining room having drinks, no doubt."

"Good," Luke rubbed his temples. "Drinks will most definitely be necessary."

Darcy stood in the dining room doorway with her hands clasped insecurely in front of her. In the soft candlelight, she could see her parents sitting across from each other, her mother laughing at something her father had just said. Stately and formal as the room was, you'd never know it from the reclined, casual nature of Mr. and Mrs. Fitzwilliam as they lounged lazily over martinis.

They hadn't seen Darcy standing there, and for a moment she considered turning back, but Luke was standing right behind her and she didn't want to appear weak, or let her fears show. It wasn't that she was afraid they'd be mad at her, or even disappointed; she knew she'd seen the worst of that, and that they'd be sure to be as supportive as possible after she had ended up in the hospital. What she did worry about was that they'd have nothing to talk to Luke about, that the words they spoke to him and he to them would be lost in translation, and that it would be one of the many things to scare him away. But he'd been under their roof since late last night, and though the house was big, she was sure they would suspect it by now. It was time to be an adult and face the awkwardness.

Darcy cleared her throat. Mr. and Mrs. Fitzwilliam looked up from their conversation.

"Darling, hi!" Mrs. Fitzwilliam beamed. "Come join us."

"And bring that young man hiding behind you," Mr. Fitzwilliam joked. "Come on in, Luke. We don't bite."

"Good evening, sir," Luke said stiffly, joining Darcy at the table.

"No need to be so proper, Luke," Mrs. Fitzwilliam assured him. "You can relax. You're welcome here."

"That's . . . great to hear." He sat stiffly in his chair. Darcy stifled a laugh—she couldn't help but be amused by his palpable discomfort. A maid, one Darcy didn't recognize, came by and poured water into glasses for Darcy and Luke.

"Thank you." Darcy nodded her appreciation, and Luke followed suit.

"Wine?" asked Mrs. Fitzwilliam.

"No, thank you," said Darcy.

"Yes, please," said Luke, simultaneously.

Mr. Fitzwilliam chuckled.

"Greta," he addressed the maid. "Will you bring Mr. Bennet a glass of the Chianti?"

"Certainly, Mr. Fitzwilliam."

The group sat in silence as Greta left and returned with a glass of bloodred wine for Luke. Darcy waited for him to take a sip, then she launched in, driven and cutthroat as if it were a business meeting and time was money. "So. As you probably guessed by now, Luke and I are dating. Thank you for letting us stay here last night—or, I mean, I don't know if you knew that we were here, but if you did, thank you for not throwing us out. And if you didn't know any of this, well, now you do, and I'm not sure why I felt I needed to ramble like this, but there, now that information is out on the table."

"Darcy," Mr. Fitzwilliam said, "this is as much your home as it is ours. And you don't have to ask permission to have a guest over. You are a fully grown woman after all."

"Oh." She blushed, feeling an odd combination of relief and embarrassment. How could she have forgotten the fundamental truth that she was no longer a child in her parents' home but a grown woman with a career and a Manhattan loft and even a new *boyfriend*? "Thanks, Dad." She took a sip of her ice water.

"Now that we have all that settled"—Mr. Fitzwilliam folded his hands flat against the tabletop—"when's the wedding?"

Darcy spat out her water. She watched Luke's eyes bulge from his skull, and she was sure hers were doing the same. She laughed nervously.

"The what?" she asked.

"The wedding, of course," he repeated. "When are you thinking you'd like to have it?"

"Why . . . uh . . ." Luke stuttered. "Why would there be a wedding? I mean . . . we only just—"

"Well, you both called off engagements. I assumed that meant you were sure about each other being the one."

"Otherwise, why would you make such big decisions?" added Mrs. Fitzwilliam.

"I . . . I can't speak for Luke," Darcy spoke slowly, her head still spinning, "but in my case, calling off the engagement to Carl was actually just undoing a really big, really wrong decision."

"It was the same thing for me." Luke nodded ardently. "I felt pressured to marry Charlotte even though I knew it wasn't the right choice. Once I realized it was the wrong decision and that I was doing it for all the wrong reasons, I had to call it off."

"Right . . ." Mrs. Fitzwilliam tilted her head to one side. "And it was your feelings for each other that made you realize you were making the wrong decisions."

"Partially, yeah, but—"

"I guess we just don't understand why you'd want to wait." Mrs. Fitzwilliam giggled. "You're obviously crazy about each other."

Maybe she's drunk, Darcy thought, hopefully. *Maybe they're both drunk and don't really mean what they're saying.*

"The Plaza is still an option, if you want to do a New York wedding," her dad continued, much to her dismay. "But, of course, there are plenty of options right here in Pemberley as well."

"Now, do you think you'll be moving back to Pemberley, darling?" her mom asked. "Or Luke, will you be moving to New York? I personally think you should settle in Pemberley; it's a much finer place to raise kids, after all."

The word *settle* paired with the word *kids* made Darcy lightheaded. She didn't mean to, but she snapped.

"None of this matters right now," she blurted dramatically, startling the whole table, Luke included. "Today is literally the first day of our relationship. We're taking things slowly, and quite frankly it's none of your business anyway." She felt her cheeks grow hot and her throat close up.

"Now, Darcy," Mr. Fitzwilliam said gently, "take a deep breath. We don't want you fainting again."

He was right; this wasn't worth another hospital visit. She took a deep breath and tried to tell herself that there was no pressure, that she and Luke could move at their own pace, that china patterns and venue scouting could be safely in the distance if she wanted them to be.

"Excuse me," she said. "I need to get some fresh air."

She scooted her chair out and hurried back through the doorway, scampering up one flight of stairs to the top-floor balcony. She pushed open the French doors and breathed in the fresh, icy air. Seconds later, Luke appeared next to her.

"You can't just leave me alone with them!" He laughed. "That was so awkward!"

"How can you be laughing right now?" she asked, impressed with his composure. "Didn't you hear them? They're hearing wedding bells and naming grandchildren in there!"

"So? That's their problem, not ours."

"Okay, okay." She wrung her hands. "Maybe you're right."

"You never used to care what your parents thought. What changed?"

"Wrong. I always cared what my parents thought. I defied them anyway, but their disapproval tore me up inside. I just finally got their approval back. I guess I'm scared to lose it again."

"Hey . . ." He took her hands in his. "They're always going to love you, no matter what."

"You're right," she sighed. "I need to chill."

"Yes," he agreed, laughing lovingly at her. "You do."

"But how am I supposed to chill when we have big decisions to make? I mean, even if we don't plan on getting married, we have to decide if I'll move here or you'll move to New York. But let's be real. I *know* you don't want to move to New York, so that means I have to quit my job and sell my loft and—"

"Whoa, whoa, stop jumping to conclusions. I would move to

New York if you wanted me to. I'd happily move to New York or I'd happily stay here. As long as I'm with you, it doesn't matter to me."

"Seriously?" This sounded too good to be true.

"Yes, seriously."

"But your family is all here. Wouldn't you miss them?"

"Sure." He shrugged. "But I'm a grown-ass man, Darcy. I can handle it. I'll visit them and they'll come visit us in the Big Apple. It will be fine. If that's what you choose."

"So what you're saying is it's literally up to me to choose."

"Literally, yes."

"Oh boy."

"But you don't have to decide right now."

"But I kind of do! I need to let work know if I'll be back on Monday."

"Well, then, you can go back on Monday and think about what you want to do from there."

"I guess I could do that." She chewed anxiously on the cuticle hanging off the side of her thumb.

"You know what I think you need?"

"Brain surgery?"

"Very funny."

"Okay, what? What do I need?"

"A day with Bingley. Why don't you two go to the spa? You can get massages and manicures or whatever."

Darcy laughed.

"Just because he's gay doesn't mean he likes manicures," she told him.

"Sure," he said. "But Jim gets them all the time, so I assumed maybe Bingley did too."

"Jim gets manicures?"

"I know, pretty out of character, right? He's normally not into superficial stuff, but he's weirdly OCD about his nails."

"You learn something new every day. And you're right. I'm going to call Bingley. There's nothing more soothing than spa day with your bestie."

20

"Can you believe they said that?" Darcy asked. It was the next morning and she was lying next to Bingley on a lounge chair, both of them in terry cloth robes, with cucumbers over their closed eyelids.

"Well, yeah, kind of," Bingley said, taking a sip of lemon water. "They've always been kind of traditional, if not outright conservative."

"I guess you're right. I shouldn't be surprised. I guess I just thought their traditional side would want me *not* to rush into marriage. Not the other way around."

"They just want grandchildren, like all old people do," he explained. "And you're almost thirty. They don't want to die before they have a chance for you to reproduce. Or worse, stay alive long enough to see you become infertile."

"*Bingley,*" she scolded. "I'm appalled."

"*What?* It's *true.* You're not gonna be young forever. And what are you waiting for, anyway? Just get a ring on it and start popping out them babies."

"Oh really? And what about you? When are you having kids?"

"Um, I know you weren't a biology major or anything, but maybe you've heard that two men can't make a baby?"

"So? You can adopt. And you should adopt. Do you have any idea how many kids are out there who need homes?"

"I see what you're doing. We are not making this conversation about me."

"Fine. Let's just be quiet and enjoy the pleasure of doing absolutely nothing."

"Fine with me. What's on the nothingness agenda?"

"I booked massages in fifteen minutes, and then cinnamon body scrubs right after that. Then I was thinking we could do some sauna time."

"Ugh, yes," he said emphatically. "My pores need so much help."

"Let's get you a facial too, then."

"Not gonna say no to that."

"Didn't think you would."

"Hey, can I ask you something?"

"As long as it's not about marriage or babies or buying a house in Pemberley freaking Ohio."

"It's not," Bingley said, somewhat delicately.

"Then shoot."

"Does it bother you at all that Luke said . . . you know?"

"No, what?" Darcy said, though she had more than a clue what he was talking about.

"All that stuff about you being a snob and thinking that you're better than everyone else. I mean, don't get me wrong, he's obviously crazy about you, but I just keep thinking about it, about what a jerk he was to you that night."

"What are you saying?"

"I don't know. I guess that I hope he's apologized."

"Of course he's apologized. And he doesn't feel that way anymore, remember? I told you the whole story about how—"

"I know, I know," he said. "You're right. I shouldn't have brought it up. I'm sorry."

"Yeah," she said, rolling her eyes, which was a bit of a challenge beneath the cucumbers. "Maybe you shouldn't have."

"Darcy Fitzwilliam?" A masseuse in a black clinical outfit with the words "Oasis Day Spa" embroidered above a breast pocket came out from behind a curtain. "It's time for your massage."

"Perfect." Darcy sipped from her water and stood up, careful to keep the robe closed as she stood.

"See you on the other side," said Bingley.

"See ya," said Darcy, with a hint of bitterness.

As she lay in the cool dimness of massage room A, the recorded sounds of waves washing over her, her thoughts returned to what Bingley had said. It was true, Luke had called her a snob, among other things, but he didn't think that way about her anymore, did he?

"How's the pressure?" the masseuse asked in a soft, melodic voice as she kneaded the knots in Darcy's tense back muscles.

"It's great, thanks," Darcy murmured. She wanted to add,

"The pressure of life, however, is not so great," but decided against it.

You're a snobby New Yorker. She heard Luke's voice from that night, saying those words that had shocked and crushed her. She rocked her head from side to side, trying to get the voice out of her head.

You're so obsessed with yourself. There it was again. When she had returned to New York after he said those things, she had buried the memory, pushed it out of her mind, but Bingley had unlocked the box, and now the experience of standing, cold and vulnerable, in the Bennet living room was flooding out.

You don't know what love is.

All you're thinking about is yourself.

You should go back to the city and leave me alone.

You're even worse than I thought.

Darcy squeezed her eyes shut, as if this would chase away the flashes of unwanted memory, but they only grew louder. As much as she now wanted to, she couldn't pretend it hadn't happened. *But he apologized,* she told herself, *and he took it all back, so why are you getting so bent out of shape about this?*

"Excuse me?" she asked the masseuse. "Do you know which room my friend is getting his massage in?"

"Um, yes," the masseuse replied, confused. "He should just be in the room next door."

"Great." Darcy began to sit up, then stopped herself. "Would it be snobby and selfish and, like, inconsiderate of me if I interrupted this for just one second to go ask him something?"

"Snobby and selfish in what way?" the masseuse asked. "And inconsiderate to whom?"

"Oh," thought Darcy. "Well, I guess to you."

"You're paying me, and this is your massage, so all you're interrupting is your own massage time."

"Interesting."

"I suppose it might be inconsiderate to interrupt your friend's massage, especially if he's enjoying it."

"Oh, I'm paying for his entire spa day. He'll survive."

"Well then . . ." The masseuse smiled, clearly amused. "I'll wait right here."

"Bingley!" Darcy swung open the door of the adjacent room. Bingley was lying on his stomach with nothing but a tiny towel covering his butt.

"Darcy, what the hell?"

"Excuse me, miss, but—"

"It's okay, Glenda," Darcy said, reading the tag on the masseuse's lapel. "I'm paying for all this. And I tip really well. Will you just give us a moment?"

"Uh . . . sure." Glenda wiped the oil from her hands.

"Again, let me repeat: Darcy, what the hell?"

"You're the one who put those thoughts of what Luke said to me back in my head, so now you're the one who is going to help me figure them out."

"What are you even talking about?" Bingley sat up and pulled his terry cloth robe off of a hook and onto his body.

"You reminded me of all those horrible things Luke said to me, and now I can't get them out of my head. But the thing is, I can't figure out why." Darcy sat down on a black leather stool. "It shouldn't matter anymore."

"Okay . . ." Bingley scratched his head. "Why shouldn't it matter anymore?"

"Because he apologized for them. And he acknowledged that I've changed. So I shouldn't care anymore; what's passed is passed, right? Ugh, this is so annoying. When did my life become a game of Whac-A-Mole?"

"Whac-A-Mole?"

"Yes, when I've moved on from one problem another one pops up right in its place. I was stressed about my parents wanting me to get married, and as soon as I settled down about that, this thing with Luke decides to start haunting me. Partially your fault, but you were right to bring it up."

"I wish I hadn't."

"But you did. So now help me."

"Oh boy. Well, I guess if this massage isn't happening . . ."

"It'll happen. It will be your reward for helping me."

"Fine." He glared playfully at her. "Do you want to know what I think?"

"Obviously."

"I think what he said is bothering you because, even if he apologized for it, he still meant it when he said it. So, at one point in time, not too long ago, he perceived you as being a snobby elitist without a heart."

"He didn't say the 'without a heart' thing." She chewed on a fingernail.

"Not explicitly, but basically."

"Sure, but—"

"And listen to me, Darcy . . ." Bingley sat up straight and took a more serious tone. "I've known you for a long time, and I'd like to think I'm one of your best friends—"

"You're my only best friend."

"Right," he went on. "And as your best friend, I gotta say, you're not a snob."

"Well, not anymore. I've been trying to change, after he said those things."

"No, Darcy, I'm saying that you've never been a snob. I'm saying that Luke or anyone else who ever thought that about you is wrong."

"What?" She laughed. "But everyone thinks I'm a snob. I'm rich as hell and I'm pretty and I'm smart and I grew up super-privileged and I never date because none of the men I meet are good enough for me and—"

"Okay, but, Darcy, see, none of those things mean you're a snob. And none of those things mean you only care about your-self. You're privileged, yes, but that's not your fault, and it's not a sin or a crime to be driven and aim for success, nor is it a crime to achieve that success."

"Hmm." She thought this over. He had a point. She couldn't blame herself for her genes and her goals, and maybe if other people did, then that was on them, not her. "But what about me thinking I'm too good for everyone?"

"Do you really, though? You don't go on dates because the men you meet are creepy Wall Street losers and you have enough self-esteem to know not to waste your time with them. It's not that you think you're too good for everyone, it's that you have confidence and think highly of yourself, which you should, because you're incredible."

Oh my God, Darcy thought, *he's right. Luke misunderstood my self-esteem for snobbery. He judged me. No, worse, he prejudged me. He assumed he knew me but he didn't. He labeled me and wrote me off. If anything, he's the snob. The kind of snob who thinks he's better than everyone because of the very fact that he goes around acting like he's not better than everyone. God,* she thought, *that's the worst kind of snob there is.*

"Bingley, you're so right," she said. "He was wrong about me. He made me feel like a bad person, but I'm not a bad person."

"No, you're a good person. You've always been a caring friend, and you rushed home to be with your mom as soon as you found out about the heart attack, didn't you? If you ask me, that sounds like the opposite of snobby and selfish."

"You're right!" She found herself growing simultaneously excited and indignant. "And I give so much money to charities! And I volunteer at homeless shelters on my time off."

"Do you really?"

"Sometimes," she admitted. "I want to do it more, though."

"Admirable," Bingley agreed.

"Luke didn't take any of these things into consideration. All he knew was that I hold myself in high regard, and he interpreted that . . . negatively. He saw my self-esteem and was . . . repulsed by it." She mulled this new version of reality over in her mind. The more she thought about it, the more unnerved she became.

"Okay, well, hold on, let's not go that far. We don't want to jump to conclusions," said Bingley.

"So what are you saying we should do?"

"I don't think there's a *we* in this, but I think you should talk to him. Calmly. There's plenty of time in relationships to voice your concerns. Trust me."

"But that's just the thing," Darcy went on. "Do I want to be in a relationship with someone who has so poorly misjudged me?"

"Do you . . . think he understands that he misjudged you?"

"I honestly don't know. Now I'm starting to think that if he ever thought I was snobby and selfish, he still thinks I'm snobby and selfish."

"Maybe. But again, all you have to do is talk—"

"The only thing that 'changed his mind' about me was that I basically bought his brothers out of juvenile hall. And quite frankly, even though my heart was in a good place when I did it, I don't think it's exactly the most noble or awesome thing I've done, by any means. I don't know if I'm even proud of it, to be honest."

"Why wouldn't you be? You got them out of some seriously hot water."

"But what if they deserved to be in that hot water? . . . Sorry, that sounded callous. What I meant was, what if they needed to learn the hard way in order to straighten out? They're pretty gnarly kids, from what I hear, and they don't have any reason to change their ways, now that I swooped in and essentially made it so that they can act however they want and not get punished for it."

"Darcy, you are hilarious. Please, let's deal with one issue at a time. If you're really worried about that, you can go back to Principal Whatever-Her-Name-Is and renegotiate."

"Okay. Like, how?"

"I don't know," he laughed. "Maybe you can pay for them to go to one of those fancy wilderness camps where they can learn how to be respectable humans, or something like that. But that's not the number one priority here. In the meantime, all you need to focus on is talking to Luke about his feelings. Try to give him the benefit of the doubt."

"Oh, no, no, no. Now you want me to give him the benefit of the doubt? What about in the waiting room, when you had to go and bring all this stuff up in the first place? The time for giving him the benefit of the doubt is over, buddy. The truth of the matter is that, number one, he doesn't like my confidence, which is basically the essence of who I am, and that, number two, deep down he thinks I'm a snob." She took a deep breath and looked up at Bingley, who was looking at her with a mixture of amusement, concern, and irritation. "And that, number three, if deep down he thinks I'm a selfish snob, then this is going to become a problem again in our relationship. He'll just keep making me prove over and over again that I'm not a selfish snob, when really he should be the one proving to me that he's not an arrogant jerk."

She put her hands on her hips in an attempt to regain a sense of feeling in control and grounded. Never in her whole life had she felt so unhinged, so untethered from herself, so insecure. Her anger and confusion glazed over into sadness. This wasn't how she wanted to start a relationship.

"Darcy, all I ever meant to do by bringing this up is to make sure you're not blinded by the light. It's not a big deal. It's always good to check in with your partner to make sure you're on the same page, and sometimes that has to happen in order to realize you're just not. What you shouldn't do is ruin this whole thing by attacking him or turning on him before you even have a conversation with him. Have a conversation, Darcy. Give him a chance."

"Okay." She sighed.

"Okay. Are we done here?"

"Yes."

"Then can Glenda come back now? I think my muscles are more tense than they've ever been."

21

"Are you sure you're all right?" Luke asked from across the table. He and Darcy were sitting down to dinner at Ruth's Chris Steak House and she was having a hard time keeping her new-found resentment from spreading out across her face like a bad rash.

Stay calm, she told herself. *Give him the benefit of the doubt. Just have a civil conversation with him, like Bingley said, and everything will be fine.*

"Mm-hm." She smiled with her lips pressed tightly together and opened up the menu. "Do you think we should order appe-tizers?"

"Sure. It's just that you've seemed pretty moody since I picked you up . . . and you wouldn't kiss me when I tried to kiss you. If something is bothering you, you can tell me."

Just tell him, she tried to command herself. *Say it as calmly as possible, but just say it. If you keep saying nothing is wrong, he's going to think it's worse than it is. You'll make this into a bigger thing.*

"I'm just hungry," she said, against her best judgment. "You know how I can get when my blood sugar is low."

"Sure," he said, sounding confused and disappointed. He picked up the menu and began looking it up and down.

Dammit, Darcy, she cursed herself, *why are you being like this?* She tried to find something on the menu but couldn't focus. Her mind was filling up with several different voices: one that told her to tell Luke how she was feeling, one that told her to end the relationship now and walk away, one that told her to protect her heart by any means necessary, and one that angrily judged each of these options for their flaws, shortcomings, and potential to cause her pain.

"Hi, I'm Amy and I'll be your server for tonight." A peppy blond woman approached their table. "Can I get you started with some drinks?"

"Uh, yeah," Luke said, caught slightly off guard. "Can I have a Stella Artois, please?"

"Certainly. And for the lady?" Amy turned her attention to Darcy.

"I'll have the blueberry mojito," she said quickly. Not having the wherewithal to make an intentional choice, she picked the first drink she saw.

"Awesome," said Amy. "Those will be right out."

"I didn't know you drank mojitos," said Luke.

"There's a lot you don't know about me," she replied coolly.

"What's that supposed to mean?"

"It means maybe you weren't looking at me close enough to know that I like mojitos. Maybe you assumed I'm a martini-only kind of girl, without taking the time to really get to know what type of drinks I like or don't like."

Of course, this was nonsense, and completely pointless to say, because Darcy was in no way a mojito type of girl. In fact, she didn't like any type of drink that was too sweet or too bubbly, and anybody who knew her at all would know that.

You're being psycho, she told herself. *If you can't be a responsible adult about this whole thing, then you should get out of here before you make a scene.* She'd always had such impressive self-control and couldn't understand why it had suddenly vanished. She wondered how she could get it back, then wondered *if* she could get it back or if it was gone forever.

"Whoa." He leaned back as if he'd been pushed. "Something is up with you, and you're going to tell me. I don't deserve to be spoken to like that. If you're unhappy, tell me why. Otherwise, please cut it out."

"Cut it out?" she snapped. "Don't talk to me like that. I'm not a child."

"Then why are you acting like one?"

"I'm not," she insisted, though she knew she was. Her frustration level was now so high that she felt on the verge of ripping off a piece of bread and throwing it at him.

"Clearly something is on your mind, but instead of telling me what it is, you're being silently bitter and snarky. I'm not trying to be a jerk. I just wish you'd be up front with me."

"Well, if you're not trying to be a jerk, then you've failed." She darted her eyes away from his so that he couldn't see she was on the verge of tears.

"Are you going to make me guess what this is about?"

"No. You know what, Luke—"

"Is it about what your parents said? I thought we decided we weren't going to let that get to us."

"It's not about that," she snapped.

"Oh, so it *is* about something."

"*Obviously.*" She knew it wasn't fair, but at this point she was becoming irritated that he hadn't been able to figure it out for himself. On top of everything, was he also dumb?

"Wow." He was looking at her as though she were a wild zoo animal let loose from her cage. "Hold on. You're acting hormonal. What is this *really* about?"

Dammit, Luke, she thought, *you really shouldn't have said that. Anything but that. Now things are going to get ugly.* She felt like the Hulk, triggered and unstoppable.

"Are you kidding me?" She gawked mockingly.

"Oh boy, here we go."

He doesn't deserve this. Go home before it's too late.

"You think just because I'm upset about something it has to be because I'm hormonal? You don't think I could have an actually valid reason to be upset?"

"You could, Darcy, but you won't tell me what it is."

"We're in public. I don't want to make a scene."

"You've already made a scene."

Darcy's mouth puckered. He was right and she knew it. She was losing her composure and spiraling out of control. She didn't recognize herself anymore. *Maybe this actually is hormonal,* she thought, *but it feels so much deeper than that.*

"I have to go." She stood up, teary eyed. "I can't do this right now."

"Darcy, I'm starting to get worried."

"There's nothing to be worried about. Just leave me alone and forget about having a future with me."

She turned and hurried out the front door, simultaneously hoping and not hoping that he'd follow her out. He didn't.

Makeup running down her cheeks, Darcy unlocked the door to her childhood home, ran up the staircase, and threw herself down on her bed. She didn't care that the mascara would stain her satin sheets; she buried her face deeper and deeper into them until the world faded away and all she could hear were the sounds of her own muffled sobs.

When she was finished crying, she sat up, grabbed Little Lion off the shelf, and held him close to her chest. She thought about herself just a short month and a half ago. She was living comfortably in New York, enjoying her own company and the many rare pleasures of being an independently wealthy woman. She didn't have anyone special in her life and therefore didn't have anyone she felt she had to please. She could do whatever she wanted, whenever she wanted, and she almost never cared what people thought about her. She had virtually forgotten that Luke even existed, and had almost completely given up on the idea of her father ever forgiving her or approving of her actions. How had so much changed in such a short amount of time? What if her mother hadn't had a heart attack—would Darcy still be complacent in New York, trudging ahead with her role as partner in one of New York's most successful hedge fund companies?

She knew there was no use in speculating, but either way, she had to get a grip, and in order to get a grip, she would have to understand why she lost her grip. As a logical person, she felt inclined to buy a bulletin board and map out the clues and evidence she had so far, the way Claire Danes does in *Homeland*, but decided it was ridiculous to take something this ridiculous so seriously. When she was growing up and had a problem that needed solving, she used to go on walks in the expansive Fitzwilliam garden, and now that seemed like the only possible thing that could begin to cheer her up. She dried her eyes, bundled herself up, and headed out for the garden.

Like the Fitzwilliam home itself, the Fitzwilliam garden was famous in the neighborhood for being the largest and the most beautiful. It dipped down in a grassy knoll behind the mansion and then stretched out in seven acres of lush greenery. The garden had been first planted and groomed in the 1960s, way before Darcy was born, and had grown and developed into a wonderland of apple trees and baby's breath and honeysuckle and lavender and elaborately geometric topiary and ivy growing up a gazebo made of glass. As kids, she and her brothers would play hide-and-seek among the topiary. But hide-and-seek was her least favorite game, so while the "It" person counted to twenty, Darcy would sneak away to the gazebo and lock herself in, then lie down on one of the benches and look up at the clouds, watching the wind blow them gently past her glass roof. The gazebo was off limits, so nobody would think to look for her in there, and the garden was so big that the boys could hunt and hunt for hours before suspecting that Darcy had fled the game entirely. Then the sun would set and Mrs. Fitzwilliam would call them in for dinner, and Kenneth would call out, "Okay, Darcy, you win. Come out, wherever you are. It's time for dinner."

202 ★ MELISSA DE LA CRUZ

She'd wait five minutes after that, until she was sure everyone was inside, and then she'd make her way out of the gazebo and indoors for dinner, proud of herself that nobody knew her hiding spot. The secret was that the gazebo was such an obvious hiding spot that nobody thought to look there.

Now it was a winter night, and so there were no clouds to gaze up at, only one never-ending blanket of dark purple-gray. Darcy strolled through the garden, hoping that focusing on its many eccentricities and attractions would calm her mind, and maybe provide her with some answers. As she walked she became more and more confident that if she cleared her mind, the answers would come.

She arrived at the gazebo and pulled open the iron-rimmed door. If the night air was chilly, the inside of the gazebo was freezing, but Darcy didn't mind. Her brain had always felt sharpest in the cold. She flipped on the light switch and could see her shivering reflection in every pane of glass. She sat down on one of the benches and curled her knees up into her chest.

Can't I just stay like this forever? she wondered. *Couldn't I curl up here and hide out for a while? Would anyone really notice I was gone? I could say I'm going on vacation but just stay right here, instead.* This seemed like a much easier, more appealing option than having to come out and face the world, having to parse this whole mess with Luke, having to deal with how horrible everything felt.

Just then, she heard a noise. It was a rustling in the topiary. Her heart skipped a beat. *It's just a squirrel,* she told herself. *Ignore it.* But then came the footsteps. They pattered down the cobblestone pathway she had just walked down, and they were approaching the gazebo. *Oh my God, did somebody follow me?* Her heart thumped in her chest. *I shouldn't have come out here alone at night,* she thought, rushing up to make sure the gazebo door was locked.

The person to whom these footsteps belonged came closer and turned the knob of the gazebo door. Darcy relaxed her shoulders slightly, knowing that as long as this person didn't have the nerve to break the glass, then she was safe. And if they *did* have the nerve to break the glass, she knew the alarm would go off and the police would be there in minutes. But, to her shock and dismay, she heard the sound of jingling keys, and then the sound of a key sliding into a lock.

She backed up, looking around for a place to hide, but there was none. She felt the blood drain from her face as she watched the knob turn. Thinking as quickly and rationally as she could, Darcy pulled off one of her Steve Madden kitten heels and prepared to throw it. The door opened, and in that exact moment she threw her shoe so that it hit the intruder's head.

"*Agh-h-h!*" Darcy's mom shrieked, stumbling backward.

"*Mom?*" Darcy panted.

"*Darcy?* What in God's name is going on? Did you just throw your shoe at me?"

"Oh my God!" Darcy ran to her mom. "I am so sorry. I thought you were an intruder."

"*An intruder with a key?*" Now that her mother had said it, Darcy realized how absurd her line of thinking had been. If it had been an intruder, somebody who had seen her and followed her home, he (or she) wouldn't have a key.

"That's a good point." Darcy's cheeks reddened.

"Who would even be intruding? We haven't ever had an intruder."

"I don't know . . . I didn't think about it. I was blinded by fear! Plenty of people must be after our money, aren't they?"

"Well, if they are they certainly aren't going hunting for it in the gazebo."

"Another good point," Darcy had to admit.

"And our security system is state of the art, you know that. Nobody can get back here without the pass code to the gate. And if someone tried to jump the fence, an alarm would go off instantly. Not to mention the security cameras. Didn't you think of that?"

"I wasn't thinking at all," Darcy admitted, which was ironic, since the reason she had embarked on this walk in the first place was to think. "Mom, I can't believe I hit you. I am so, so sorry. What were you even doing back here?"

"I was taking my nighttime stroll and I saw that the gazebo light was on. I thought I must have left it on earlier by accident. I wasn't expecting to get hit by a shoe."

"I'm so embarrassed." Darcy hid her face in her hands.

"That's okay." Mrs. Fitzwilliam looked quizzically at her daughter. "I know it wasn't on purpose. But Darcy . . . are you all right? You're shaking."

Darcy looked down at her hands and saw that they were, in fact, trembling.

"I don't know," she said, being honest for the first time that day. "I don't know if I'm okay."

"Sit down, darling." Mrs. Fitzwilliam held Darcy's hand and

they sat down together on the bench. "Tell me what's going on. Is it Luke?"

"Yes." Darcy sighed.

"What did he do? I knew he was too rough around the edges for my daughter."

"I don't know, Mom. I don't think it's all his fault. It's kind of a long story."

"Well, I don't have anywhere to be, do you?"

"I guess not."

"Then let's talk it out."

Darcy couldn't remember the last time she had a true heart-to-heart with her mom. She barely knew where to begin. She told of how she'd first come to realize that she was in love with Luke, how she went to his house and professed her love in a completely inappropriate display of romance. She told of how he not only had shot her down but also had attacked her character, and how she had taken his word for gospel, taken it to heart and believed that she was a selfish person who needed to change her ways. She told her mom about Kit and Lyle and how she saved them from being shipped away to juvenile hall, and how she was dehydrated and she'd forgotten to eat for too long and ended up in the hospital. She told of how she'd rushed to Luke's engagement party, only to find that it was canceled, and how he'd changed his mind about her after learning what she'd done for his brothers. She told of how happy they'd been to finally be together, and of how it lasted barely a day before things had unraveled right before her eyes.

"Oh, honey," Mrs. Fitzwilliam said. "We didn't mean to put any unnecessary stress on you. You know we only want you to be happy. We get carried away, but all you have to do is say, 'Mom, Dad, back off,' and we'll back right on off. Sometimes we just need to be reminded."

"Well, thanks. But then I went to Oasis Spa with Bingley and he reminded me of what Luke had said, and then I just couldn't get it out of my mind. So I planned to get dinner with Luke and tell him how uncomfortable I was and how I couldn't get the memory of him calling me selfish out of my head, but when I got to dinner, no matter how hard I tried, I couldn't be honest. I wanted to be honest, I really did, but instead I got bratty and moody and completely shut down. Then I ran home and cried, and I thought if I came out to the garden I could think more clearly, and . . . well, you know the rest."

"Yes," Mrs. Fitzwilliam chuckled. "The part where you threw a shoe at my head and nearly gave me a concussion."

"How can you joke about that? And in a time like this, when your only daughter is clearly having a nervous breakdown?"

"Honey . . ." She chuckled again. "You're not having a nervous breakdown."

"I'm not?"

"No, you're not. In fact, it makes perfect sense that you're reacting this way."

"It does?"

"Isn't it obvious? The last time you were open and honest with him about how you felt, he rejected your feelings and he attacked your character! Of course you're afraid to open up to him again; you don't want to get hurt again."

Darcy stared at her mother, blinking. She was right. This *was* obvious. Only Darcy had been too frantic to see it. She couldn't bring herself to tell him how she felt this time because last time she got so hurt. Her body was literally shutting down as a way to protect herself from getting hurt again.

"Shutting down has always been easier than being vulnerable." She hadn't meant to say it out loud, but she was glad she had, so she could hear it in her own voice.

"That's exactly right, darling."

"So what do I do?"

"That's entirely up to you."

"But I don't even know my options!"

Mrs. Fitzwilliam laughed again at her daughter, prompting Darcy to laugh along with her; she was gradually feeling less and less panicked.

"You can tell Luke your concerns and risk getting hurt, or stay emotionally shut down and most definitely stay in pain, because you will have destroyed a potentially good thing."

"So I'll get hurt either way?"

"The first way you might get everything—relief from this anxiety and the love of your life back."

"Do you really think he could be the love of my life?"

"I don't know, darling," she said. "But there's really only one way to find out."

22

Mrs. Fitzwilliam brought a pot of chamomile tea to Darcy's room, which she sipped gratefully, sitting in her reading nook, looking up at the twinkling stars. When she felt ready, Darcy picked up her phone and opened up the text app.

No, she told herself, *don't send a text. Call him. This isn't high school.*

She clicked on his name and hit the Call button, then listened anxiously while it rang. She put the call on speakerphone and held it away from her ear so that it didn't feel so intense. Would he be mad? Defensive? Would he even answer? When he answered, her heart skipped a beat.

"Hello?" he said.

"Hi, Luke, it's Darcy."

"I know." He sounded tired, like maybe he had been asleep.

"Oh, right, okay," she stammered. "Look, I don't know how mad at me you are for the way I acted tonight, but if you'd give me a chance, I'd like to explain everything that's been going on with me."

For a moment, only silence came from the receiver. Darcy closed her eyes and swallowed. Maybe this relationship wouldn't work out, but it would crush her to know that she was the one who ruined it.

"Where do you want to meet?" he said, clearing his throat.

She hadn't thought about it; she'd figured they'd talk on the phone.

"Oh, uh . . ."

"How about we get mojitos at the Tiki Room?" he joked dryly.

She laughed. *Okay*, she breathed, *maybe we can recover from this*.

"I actually kind of like that idea," she said. "See you there in thirty?"

"Okay, Darcy," he said. "Whatever you want."

She got there early and ordered herself a drink. The Tiki Room was, as it sounded, a tropical-themed bar adorned with tiki faces etched into the wood, plastic palm trees, a green, jungle-esque glow, and electric tiki torches perched in every corner. She was only partly surprised when the bartender poured her drink into a hollowed-out pineapple and stuck it with a tiny paper umbrella. She asked for a Stella Artois for Luke, then paid the bartender and took the drinks to a booth in the way back, where the wall was covered in plastic bamboo entangled with red and green Christmas lights that hadn't yet been taken down.

Luke arrived right on time, sliding into the vinyl seat across from her. Between them was a map of Hawaii, stuck beneath a layer of Plexiglas. "Kokomo" by the Beach Boys started to play.

"This place is really weird," he said.

"You picked it."

"I was joking."

"Thank you for meeting me," she said. "I didn't want to make you come out again so late."

"I don't mind," he said. "It sounded important. No mojitos?"

"Well, I guess that's a good place to start. I have to be honest with you: I hate mojitos and I always have. So when you said you didn't think I was a mojito kind of girl, you were actually spot on."

"So you gaslit me."

"I what?"

"You made me think I was wrong and crazy for thinking something, even though it was completely accurate."

"Yes, exactly, and I'm really sorry for that—"

"I don't understand. Why did you pretend you like mojitos?"

"I'm getting to that part."

"Okay . . ."

"I pretended to like mojitos and was an overall asshole to you at dinner because I wanted to tell you something but was afraid of how you'd react."

"That's what I thought," he said. "God, glad I'm not crazy. But why couldn't you just tell me?"

"Because last time I told you how I felt you shot me down. You called me a snob and—"

"But you know I didn't mean it!"

"That's the thing; I don't know that. The morning when you

said those things, you were just so sure, so convinced that I was a spoiled and entitled brat. And as far as I can tell, the only thing that changed your mind was that I bought your brothers a Get Out of Jail Free card, and for no other reason than to prove to you that I am in fact a good person who thinks of other people. If anything, it was one of the more self-centered things I've done, especially since I didn't consider if it was even what was best for your brothers."

"You did the right thing," he said. "Juvie is a hellhole, and—"

"Okay, maybe. But you thought of me as a snob before that, and if that's really the only thing that made you change your mind, then, I mean, what's stopping you from going right back to seeing me that way again? Maybe I'll send back my meal at dinner or I'll want our kids to go to private school and you'll interpret that as snobby and you will judge me. And what I realized, what really started to bug me, was that the truth is I'm not all that snobby and I'm not really selfish. You perceived me that way, you interpreted my actions as snobby for all these years, even though I'm actually a pretty good person and you never saw that until I bailed your brothers out. And I don't know what to do with that information, but it was sitting really badly with me, and I wanted to express all this to you, and I know I should have sooner, but I didn't want . . . I didn't want to get hurt again."

"Are you finished?" he asked.

"Yes." She took a moment to catch her breath.

"I am sincerely so sorry for what I said that night. The real, honest-to-God truth is that I don't, and never did, think poorly of you. Now, if you'll let me, I'd really love to explain what happened."

"Oh." Darcy was surprised. "Yes. Of course."

"I'd been dating Charlotte for a little over three years. Things were great, we had a lot of good times and we got along really well, no fighting or anything like that. My parents were crazy about her and said from the beginning that I should marry her, but something about that plan didn't feel quite right to me. It was always a good relationship, but some things were always a little off. Like how we never really had the same sense of humor. Or, rather, she never really had any sense of humor at all. And I don't say that to be unkind, obviously. I'm just trying to help you understand how things got to be . . . well, how they were."

"Sorry to interrupt," she said. "But how does this have anything to do with you thinking or not thinking that I'm a snob?"

"It's the backstory. Key backstory. Don't worry, I'm getting to it."

"Okay." She nodded gently. "Keep going."

"So about two months ago she came to me and she said she'd been reading this book, a self-help book, that said if your boyfriend hasn't proposed after two years of dating, then you need to break up with him, because it means his heart just isn't in it."

"Oh, yikes. And you'd already been dating three years."

"Exactly. So she asked me if we're moving forward or if she's wasting her time with me, and I honestly didn't know, so I said that, and she said she was leaving me! I was a little sad, but mostly I was relieved, so I didn't try to fight her on it. She was ready for marriage and I just wasn't. Or, I think, more importantly, I wasn't ready to marry *her*."

"I see."

"Yeah, so then you showed up before Christmas and, my God, I feel bad saying this, but I practically forgot all about Charlotte. In high school I had a huge crush on you, but I always thought you were too good for me—way too smart and way too beautiful—so I never let on that I had any feelings whatsoever."

"You were a competitive jackass," she reminded him. "You unhooked my bra once during Mr. Walser's bio class."

"Right, yeah." He scratched his head and blushed. "And I'm sorry about that, but my suppressed feelings were just expressing themselves through alternative routes. Little did I know that giving a girl a hard time in high school is basically the same thing as baking her a cake that says 'I LIKE YOU' in big red letters."

"I guess figuring that out is a rite of passage."

"And I totally get why my behavior made you think of me as just another high school idiot. Anyway, I always liked you, and I loved giving you a hard time, because it was the only thing that ever made you pay attention to me. I challenged you during debate because you were the smartest girl and the funnest to argue with."

"*Most fun.*"

"What?"

"I was the most fun to argue with. You said *funnest*. But it's *most fun.*"

"Seriously, Darcy?"

"Yes, that is seriously the correct way of saying it."

"But are you seriously pointing it out in the middle of me pouring my heart out to you?"

"Yes. It makes it . . . *funner*, don't you think?"

He tried not to smile but couldn't help it.

"Very *funny*," he said. "So, like I was saying, I hadn't seen you in, like, a decade, and when I saw you all those feelings came flooding back—how beautiful you are, how frighteningly smart, how different you are from everyone else I've ever known—and I felt like I had to have you. You made me feel so many things Charlotte had never made me feel, and I just thought 'Okay, it makes sense now. How could I have wanted to marry Charlotte when I didn't feel any of this for her?'"

"And then we kissed, that night . . ." Darcy recalled.

"Yes, and I thought it was too good to be true. I thought you must have been too drunk to know what you were doing."

"Well, I was."

"But then it happened again."

"I think I was drunk then too, wasn't I?"

"Okay, great. So you never actually wanted to kiss me and we're just sitting here for no reason right now, is that what you're saying?"

"No. God, don't be such a baby. Of course I wanted to kiss you. Both times. I realized I had fallen in love with you and I tried to shake it off but I couldn't. Drunk or sober, you were suddenly always on my mind."

"And you were always on my mind," he said.

"Then what happened?"

"I was thinking about how I could take things further with you, maybe take you on an actual date so that you knew I wanted more than something drunk and casual. Charlotte came to me that night and tried to get back together. I told her I couldn't, because I had fallen for you and was going to try and pursue you. She didn't like hearing that, obviously. She got really serious and reminded me of what I suspected all along: Darcy Fitzwilliam is way too good for me."

"*She told you that?*"

"She said to get real, that a girl like you would never truly want to be with a guy like me. She told me you had to be using me as a quick distraction before going back to New York."

"But—"

"And I believed her. I believed her because I had already believed it deep down! Then she told me she had seen you talking with Carl at the Glidden House, and that you were probably getting back together."

"What the hell? Charlotte was at the—"

"I was so sure you'd be rejecting me any minute, then, and Charlotte convinced me to get out while I still could. I knew I could feel safe with Charlotte, that she would never hurt me the way you potentially could, so I chose to stay. Remember, this was when I didn't believe you could ever want to be with a guy like me."

"Wow," said Darcy. "That's . . . sad. I'm sorry you felt that way."

"Well, what I did next was probably more sad. She told me I had to cut off my relationship with you, and I agreed. I thought if I was going to have a marriage and a family with her, I was going to have to do everything I possibly could to make it work."

"I understand that . . ."

"But then you came to our house that day. I was with Charlotte, in my room. Jim came upstairs and told me—us—you were there. Charlotte told me that if I didn't go down there and tell you that you're a selfish, heartless snob and to never talk to me again, she'd leave me."

"Oh my God." Darcy gawked, reimagining that morning in the rain, now that she had this new information. "That is psychotic."

"Maybe," he agreed. "But the really psychotic thing was that I listened to her, Darcy. I went down there and gave you every reason to never talk to me again. I had to really push you away, give you a good reason to hate me. And it wasn't hard to fake it; I just channeled that inner part of me that always thought I didn't deserve you. That made me mad enough to be able to say what I said."

"Oh my God," Darcy said again. "So you didn't actually mean any of that?"

"That's what I'm saying," he said. "Not one word. I mean, that doesn't make it okay, Darcy. I still said it, and that's unforgivable. It doesn't change anything."

"Uh . . . I think it might change some things," she thought out loud. "But okay. So then I heard about Kit and Lyle and I wanted to prove to you that I'm not selfish, so I came back to Pemberley and I talked to the principal and somehow you found out what I had done, and so then . . . then what?"

"Well, then I said to Charlotte how amazing it was that you went so far out of your way to help my family. She flipped out and said, 'If Darcy is really so great, then why don't you just marry her instead?' I don't think she meant it. It was just a dramatic thing to say, and maybe I should have brushed it off more casually, but instead I said, 'I've already committed to marrying *you*.' And she snapped and said, 'Well, maybe we should call it off right now.'"

"Wow."

"Yeah, exactly, wow. So I told her that yes, I thought we should call the whole thing off after how she'd manipulated me. After, I wanted to go to go to the Tavern and drink by myself, completely haunted by the horrible things she had me say to you—and the fact that I'd agreed to say them. But then Bingley called me and told me that you were going to the party and that nobody had told you it was canceled. He said I should go apologize to you, and that you'd accept my apology if I did. So I went and I found you there, and, well, the rest is history."

"So . . . Wow . . ." She needed a moment, or seven hundred, to let all of this sink in. "So then it's true; you really don't think of me that way. You know that, even though I come off as snobby sometimes, it's really just that—"

"You're not a snob. You just respect yourself, and that can be misunderstood as snobbery to somebody who doesn't know anything about self-esteem. Probably to people who themselves have low self-esteem."

"Oh my God, exactly! That's exactly it. So you do get it."

"I get that you're incredible and never deserved to be treated how I treated you that night."

"So you truly don't think I'm a bad person," she reiterated, mostly just so she could hear it again.

"I really don't. And you . . ." he began, getting shy. "You don't think you're too good for me?"

"No." She shook her head, smiling. "I think I'm just right for you. And I think you're just right for me."

Luke pushed their drinks aside and reached over the table to kiss her. She kissed him back, feeling for the first time that everything was right and true and good.

ALMOST TWO YEARS LATER

Darcy woke to sunlight spilling in through the space between two curtains and the honking, revving, rumbling sounds of traffic down below. It was like a symphony to her. She stretched her arms and legs out wide across the California king–size bed and then plucked her newest pair of glasses off the nightstand.

Her apartment had changed so much in just two years' time. The decor that was once icy gray and modern was now warm and homey. Artful sunsets hung from the walls, and photographs of loved ones sat propped on the tabletops. The curtains, which were once gray silk, were now blue gingham. She didn't know how she had let that happen, but she had.

The smell of waffles wafted in beneath her door.

"Ooh, yay," she said out loud. "I'm starving!" She slipped a fleece robe on over her nightgown and walked out into the kitch-enette and dining area.

"Look who it is," said Luke, looking up from the waffle iron. "Sleeping Beauty." He was in a white T-shirt and boxers, his face freshly shaven.

"Thanks for letting me sleep in," she said, admiring how handsome he was. "The waffles smell great."

"You needed the rest. You haven't had a break even for a moment in months."

"I know." She yawned. "But it's all been worth it."

"Syrup?" he asked, slipping the waffle onto a blue porcelain plate.

"Yes, please. Lots."

He drizzled authentic Vermont maple syrup over the waffle, so that it flooded the square compartments and oozed off the sides. Just how she liked it: more syrup than waffle. This was also how she liked her frozen yogurt: more sprinkles than yogurt.

"Mm," she said. "Delicious."

"Glad you like it," he said, though he knew she always did. She loved practically everything he cooked for her, and she was impressed that he'd developed such a skill—and a career for himself, based on that skill—in such a short amount of time.

"Do you have a job today?" she asked.

"It's Sunday, silly," he said, joining her at the table with a hot cup of coffee.

"Even so," she said, "rich people still have to eat their per-sonally, professionally prepared meals, don't they?"

"You would know." He winked. "But yeah, they do. I just don't work Sundays, remember?"

"Oh, yeah! So glad you decided to do that."

"Me too," he said. "Now I can be with my favorite girls. What do you think we should do today? I was thinking maybe we'd take Millie to the zoo? She's never been."

"We can't," said Darcy. "We have to get ready for the flight tonight. I haven't packed at all yet."

"Oh boy," he said. "That's right. Well, she's never been on a plane before, either, so that'll be a fun first."

"I'm assuming she's still asleep," said Darcy. "I know, otherwise I would have heard the relentless jibber-jabber by now."

"She's asleep," he said. "She woke up at five in the morning but just went down for a nap about thirty minutes ago."

Darcy swiveled off her seat and went to the mesh crib set up in the center of the living room. She peered in to see her four-month-old daughter fast asleep with her thumb in her mouth and her Little Lion gripped tightly against her chest. She had pale skin and wispy, light-brown hair that barely covered her big head. Her eyes were shut tight, but when they opened they were bright emerald green, like her dad's.

When she was born, Darcy struggled to find a name. The factual way in which she'd always gone about naming stuffed animals and pets (Little Lion, Big Dog) didn't work in this scenario, though she wished it would, for the sake of convenience. She took her daughter home and called her Little Baby for as long as she could, until Luke had put his foot down and said it was time to get serious about a name. They had tried on many different names, but the truth was, neither of them knew much about girls' names. After all, both of them had only ever had brothers, and Darcy had never been the type to have many girl friends. Luke could draw from the list of girls he had dated, but obviously *that* wouldn't do.

Darcy suggested Dominique and Dagny, her two favorite heroines from Ayn Rand novels, but Luke vetoed them, saying they weren't pretty enough. Luke suggested Angelica and Eliza, the names of the sisters Alexander Hamilton was in love with, and who were in love with him. (Once they were living in New York City, Luke discovered that he loved *Hamilton*, the musical. They had been to see it three times, and he couldn't get enough.) Darcy vetoed both, saying that they were too flowery, and also that she wouldn't name her daughter after a girl who fell for a smooth talker.

"Okay then," Luke had said, "should we name her after one of our mothers?"

"I like that idea, but then whichever one we don't name her after will feel left out."

"That's true. Well . . . do you know any other women, maybe someone nonfictional, who you admire?"

"How about Millie?" Darcy suggested.

"Who's Millie?"

"My assistant. She's loyal and humble and . . . grounded. Things I want our daughter to be."

"Millie," Luke said. "I love it."

"I am in love with New York in the wintertime," Luke said, as their cab drove down Fifth Avenue. The store windows were all aglow with high-budget displays, each one a miniature production. The skinny trees that lined the sidewalk were wrapped from head to toe in white lights, and wreaths the size of small cars hung above the street, strung between buildings.

"There's nothing else like it," Darcy agreed. "Thank you for living here with me."

"It was the right choice."

"Millie . . ." Darcy spoke to her daughter, who sat bundled in her lap. "What do you think? Do you like New York?"

Millie pointed one finger into the air and said, "Bblkrrshhh."

"I think that's a yes," said Darcy.

"Me too," Luke agreed.

On the airplane, Darcy strapped Millie's car seat into one of the three first-class seats she had purchased. She and Luke sat down on either side of their daughter and held hands, so that their linked arms rested over Millie, and Darcy's wedding ring looked supernatural as it glittered beneath the soft purple overhead lights. Mild-mannered Millie fell asleep just in time for takeoff.

The ring, like almost everything else in their relationship, was part of a memorable story. It started just a month after their kiss at the tiki bar. They'd moved into Darcy's New York apartment and were settling comfortably into their new life together. It was the evening of Darcy's birthday, and they were on the train to Coney Island. When Luke had asked her what she wanted to do for her birthday, she had described the perfect night of being "normal," which for her meant "living as if I'm part of the ninety-nine percent." Luke had packed a picnic and they had mapped out the trains that would take them from the Upper East Side of Manhattan to the rickety old theme park way at the very end of

Brooklyn, where they'd play games and go on rides and, ultimately, spend the night.

"What did your parents say when you told them we'd be living together out of wedlock?" Luke asked, as the F train rocked from side to side and the fluorescent lights flickered on and off.

"I didn't tell them," Darcy confessed. "When we told them we were dating, they started asking about marriage and kids. I figured it would be best to wait until we get engaged to tell them anything. I mean, they know we're dating, but if they knew you'd moved in they'd be all over us like flies. They can't help it; they're old-fashioned."

"So you think we'll get engaged down the line?"

"I would imagine so. Don't you? We're serious about each other; that's why you moved in."

"Yeah," he said. "I imagine so. So what are we waiting for, then?"

"Uh . . ." She thought for a moment. "I guess just for you to get up the courage to ask my parents. Which, let's face it, will be never."

"Interesting," he said, smiling mischievously.

As the train got farther and farther away from the city, the train got emptier and emptier, until it was just the two of them. *That's odd,* Darcy thought. *Where is everybody?*

Just as Coney Island came into view, the big Wonder Wheel rising up out of the wooden planks, twinkling against the night sky like a trophy, the train came to a halt.

"What's going on?" she asked. The flickering lights went off and stayed off. "What the hell is happening? Luke, I'm scared."

"Don't be scared," he said. "Look up."

She looked up and, in red dotted letters, the lights spelled out "DARCY, WILL YOU MARRY ME?"

"Oh my God," she gasped, hand clapped over her mouth.

"The thing is," he said, "I already asked your parents, and not only did they give me their blessing but they also helped me plan this."

"Oh my God," Darcy said again, tears springing to her eyes. "Yes, yes. Of course I'll marry you!"

Now, as the plane prepared for landing, Darcy thought of that night in the train, which had been her happiest up to that point. That moment had lost its place as "happiest" on the night Millie had been born.

"Are you ready for this?" Luke asked, as the FASTEN SEAT BELT sign went off and the entire planeload of passengers made a mad dash for their overhead luggage. "It's almost been two years."

"I'm a little nervous," she said. "But we can handle it."

Luke held Millie in his arms as they walked the long link of tunnels and escalators to baggage claim and found Edward standing with a small poster that read "Welcome Baby Millie!"

Darcy sighed happily and threw her arms around Edward, never so glad to be landing in Pemberley. She couldn't wait to introduce her daughter to the world she came from.